I0677464

Somewhere

in

Crime

Historical mysteries

by

Central Coast Mystery Writers

Edited & Compiled by

Sue McGinty & Margaret Searles

SOMEWHERE IN CRIME
Copyright 2011 Central Coast Mystery Writers

Printed in the United States. All rights reserved. No part of this book may be reproduced in any form, except by a print or electronic reviewer who wishes to quote brief passages in connection with a review.

All characters, locations and incidents are used fictitiously, including those names that may seem familiar. Any resemblance to to actual events, locales, or persons living or dead, is entirely coincidental.

Cover Design by Liam Heckman

ISBN 978-0-9846098-4-0

Revenge Publishing
PO BOX 6787
Los Osos, CA 93402
www.revengepublishing.com

Somewhere in Crime

Historical mysteries

Revenge Publishing

Editors' Notes

In the 1950 film "All About Eve," Bette Davis as Margo Channing famously said, "Fasten your seat belts, it's going to be a bumpy night."

We suggest you do the same, for you are about to undertake a journey on a roller coaster of short fiction that delves into the mysteries of time and space—and things that go bump in the night. The Central Coast Mystery Writers would like to extend special thanks to our eagle-eyed editor, Margaret Searles.

—Sue McGinty, Anthology Editor, author of the *Bella Kowalski* mysteries.

* * * *

"Somewhere in Crime" brings you tales of murder and mystery occurring in or influenced by the past. The first Central Coast Mystery Writers Anthology since 2006, we've had time to write and collect some remarkable tales. In "The Problem With Burlesque" Victoria Heckman's theater owner wants to show those new-fangled movies. In "The SomeWhen Murder" Susan Tuttle's Skylark is snowed in, takes shelter in an old house and somehow goes back to save a life in 1886. In "Uncertain Sanctuary" Sue McGinty's Jewish girl hides out in a mysterious lighthouse on California's Central Coast before WWII. Enjoy your ramble through these tales of bygone days, dear Reader. Who knows what memories they may evoke for you?

—Margaret Searles, author of the *Mrs. Millet & Mrs. Hark* mysteries.

Passenger to Stamboul
An Imagined Journey

Paul Alan Fahey

Fall 1928
Calais, France

As the station master and the Wagon Lit porters dashed about making last minute preparations for our journey, I leaned back in the plush comfort of my sleeping compartment and let my mind wander. I thought of my stories, my fairy tales for grown-ups, and of my fictional characters and how easily they came to me, like old friends stopping by for a cup of tea and a nice, long chat.

At first, writing was something to do like playing the piano or painting a landscape, a way to cope, a diversion from the stress, confusion and loneliness that accompanied the Great War; but later it became my lifeline when I found myself alone with a daughter to raise, a mother to support and a great country house to look after. Over some time I came to realize that writing would become my profession.

Feeling a bit drowsy, I closed my eyes and drifted back in memory two years to a time I remembered only in fragments. It was 1926, early December and three months past my 35th birthday.

At first I thought it was a dream, the kind that recur over and over in one's lifetime. The images fading in and out, the sketchiness of my lost hours and days. But then, of course, it hadn't been a dream.

My London psychiatrist had called it an hysterical fugue, a wandering state followed by amnesia, the psychological stress too much to bear, my mind locking away the trauma, my body fleeing the situation, my home, my life, my world as I knew it.

The whistle shrieked as the train lurched forward waking me from my reverie. People crowded the platform. I was a foreigner here, an ordinary redheaded Englishwoman nearing middle age, dressed in a green skirt and brown jumper. A lady in a floppy, white hat looked my way, and somehow I drew comfort in pretending she had come to see me off. I smiled at her, and, to my surprise, she waved back.

As the train gained speed, I felt the power of the magnificent engine pull the cars along the rails through the darkness of the station and out into the morning light, the gold lettering below my coach window reflected in a baker's window:

SIMPLON ORIENT EXPRESS
MILAN-BELGRADE-ISTANBUL

Over the years I had come to understand how large a role fate played in my life. Unlike the characters in my mystery novels, there were simply no outlines to follow, no signposts to read along the way. Given this knowledge, I had no difficulty understanding my present predicament. I was alone, a bit terrified but also excited, travelling aboard the train of my dreams to an ancient part of the world.

I napped and woke most of the morning in tandem with the rocking motion of the cars and the occasional screeching of the brake as the train slowed for a stop. I had just pulled out an intricate piece of embroidery from my bag and had set to work when a knocking at my door disturbed me.

The conductor poked his head in, announced that the train

was full and asked if I would mind sharing my compartment with a gentleman en route to Milan.

A glance at my railway timetable revealed we would soon cross the French border, and from there it was just over two hours to that magnificent city in northern Italy. I told the conductor I would enjoy some company given my long journey to the Middle East, and with that he tipped his hat and stepped back to allow a short, elderly man to enter the coach.

Once inside, the man nodded quite formally in my direction and immediately took off his hat and overcoat, and then stowed them along with a small briefcase and black leather valise in the rack above his head.

He pulled at the knees of his tweed trousers and slowly lowered himself onto the plush velvet upholstery opposite me. He then withdrew a slim volume from his coat pocket, the words *Das Psychoanalytische* clearly visible in the title, and holding the book close to his face, he began to read intently.

An express train moving in the opposite direction raced by, the vibration shaking the coach, its warning signal wailing, coming within inches of a devastating collision. I looked out and saw my reflection in the windows of the neighbouring cars and, as it had been in my youth when glancing at my image in the beveled mirror above my dressing table, it was as if I were looking at a stranger.

When the train passed, I returned to my sewing. Having to concentrate on the stitching of a complicated pattern had a calming effect, and coupled with the musical jogging of the train, the quick-quick-slow tempo, I began to imagine it all a rather pleasing yet very fast fox trot, the motion pulling me back to a time having no definite shape or form.

Each morning I would rise late without any enthusiasm or interest, barely reaching the chair by the large bay window. And there I would sit for hours looking down into the gardens, thinking of Mother, remembering how she had loved the roses, and how I'd looked forward to our afternoon walks. The two of us strolling together, arm in arm, planning meals, discussing my daughter's latest school project, often sharing thoughts on one of my stories.

For months my notebook lay open upon the desk, a vague outline of a jewel theft and murder aboard the Blue Train. Oh, how I grew to hate that novel, the story so sluggish, the characters a mixture of what I had written before. Yet somehow I'd gotten through it and had managed to pull a few surprises out of my hat by the denouement, but it was all a very routine affair and not one of my best efforts.

I looked up and suddenly realized my travelling companion was observing me closely. I had the oddest sensation. It felt as though his eyes had pierced my inner core, deep down to my most secret thoughts and desires. Then I stopped myself. It was mad to read too much into a look. Perhaps he had seen my photograph on the back of one of my books. European sales had increased dramatically over the past year, thanks mainly to the success of that miserable Blue Train. Or maybe, I reminded him of a friend or relative. Yes, that explanation would prove the most likely.

"*Guten Tag! Wie geht es Ihnen?*"

His deep, raspy voice startled me. "I'm sorry. I don't speak German."

"You are English then?"

"Yes, I am."

"Needlework, I think, is not good for women," he told me, while taking off his wire-rimmed spectacles and rubbing both eyes.

"I beg your pardon?" What's wrong with embroidery, I wanted to ask. Instead I averted my eyes and went back to my work, not wishing to be rude in return.

As if reading my mind, he smiled and pointed to the colorful fabric in my lap. adding, "It provides too much time for the daydreams, often with disastrous consequences."

"I disagree with you. Sewing is an art form as well as a

craft." Like painting or playing the piano, I considered it one of the true marks of a well-bred woman.

"It's a beautiful pattern that. The flowers running in circles. What do you call them in English?"

"We call them, daisies. Surely you have them in your country?"

"*Ja, naturlich.*" He looked away, turning his attention to the scenery.

The coach lights came on briefly as the train tunneled through a mountain, and then they dimmed as we returned to daylight and crossed over a trestle spanning a deep, rocky gorge.

He seemed delicate and fragile, this white-haired old man, yet at the same time quite remarkable with one hand cupped under his chin, sitting there gazing out the window, eyeglasses laying open across his knee. What an interesting personality. Perhaps in my next novel…

I pondered the idea as a host of fictional characters instantly paraded in front of me, all passengers on a train, emerging in my consciousness as if through a cloudy veil.

I saw a beautiful Hungarian Countess, a Swedish medical missionary, and a very disagreeable German businessman. No, I was being too influenced by my fellow traveller. A ruthless American with a sinister past would be a much better murder victim, and I would see to it that everyone had a motive.

I set aside the sewing and withdrew a small leather notebook from my bag. Writing quickly, I jotted down as much detail as I could remember before the images faded. I tweaked my imagination further and out popped an English governess, a British colonel returning from a post in India, a Russian princess, and an Italian-American car dealer.

The train careened around a sharp curve, and as I put down my writing materials and returned to the pattern, I knew the Orient Express would be a major character as well.

"Now do you see?" He gestured with his hand and shook his head, one eyebrow arching slightly above the other.

"I'm sorry?"

"You will say you were working hard at your task, but in fact…" and here he paused a moment with some effort as if he were translating word for word from one language to another, "you engage in an art form that propels the mind to distant places. Is that not correct?"

I looked down at the errant daisies, the yellow threads where the greens should be. I'd been woolgathering and would have to restitch that last bit. I felt foolish, but it was time to defend myself. "I am a writer, you see, and daydreaming is how I make my living."

"You work not in the real world but in the realm of make believe?"

"Yes, I suppose that's one way to put it."

"*Ja*. I guessed as much." He gave his short, gray beard a few quick tugs, and I started to laugh. I couldn't help myself. It felt good to release the tension bottled up so long inside me.

"It seems, Mrs. Christie, we have very much broken the ice." He carefully folded his glasses and slipped them into his vest pocket, and with his dark brown eyes twinkling over at me added, "And that, my dear lady, is a great improvement."

Our famous train transported us across the French border, and as we headed for the northern Italian countryside, everything fell smoothly into place. The bits and pieces like those of a jigsaw puzzle, once a jumble, were now instantly recognizable.

This man knew my identity, and I had finally placed him. For he was the famous psychoanalyst, Dr. Sigmund Freud, his face gracing countless magazine covers, his photograph featured in hundreds of newspaper articles. Despite my current circumstances and the uncertainty of what lay ahead, I found myself thinking that perhaps he was right. This might be a great improvement indeed.

* * * *

"Do you read murder mysteries, Dr. Freud?" I asked when we were comfortably seated in the dining car. The waiter had brought me a pot of Earl Grey, the doctor an espresso.

"*Ja.* I recently read one while recuperating from surgery."

This man must be very ill, I thought, and then understood why the short trip from my compartment to the dining car had seemed for him such a laborious process.

"I find your novels," he began, "as well as those of Miss Dorothy L. Sayers, such light divertissements."

* * * *

I took this as a compliment despite the left-handed manner in which it was given. One must need a break now and then from those dreary medical journals.

As our train sped along, our conversation zigzagged here and there. I spoke of my daughter who was away for the first time at boarding school. We compared travel itineraries. He was about to deliver a paper to colleagues at the Milan Psychoanalytic Institute. I told him I looked forward to visiting the architectural dig at Ur. I'd recently read about the historical findings and was anxious to see for myself an authentic excavation site.

"You are going much further than Stamboul?"

"Oh, yes," I said, "I'll only have a few hours there before resuming my journey by train to Damascus. The final leg is a bus trip across the desert to Baghdad."

"You must be keen on ancient history then."

"Very much," I said. "I plan to visit the Babylonian ruins on my way south."

"Ah, Babylon," he said, "the world's first great

civilization."

At this point, our discussion became quite lively for we had discovered a common ground, a mutual interest in the ancient world. I spoke about the pyramid-like towers of this once splendid city, now sadly reduced to hills of rubble, the debris rising above the surrounding flatlands.

"The towers were temples to the gods," he said, "built over tombs of the great kings. Many had secret chambers, not unlike those of the human mind and heart. Do you not agree?"

"I read somewhere about your interest in antiquities," I said, anxious to steer the conversation away from the personal. Pleasant though he was, the doctor was still a stranger to me, and a foreigner as well.

"*Ja*, that is correct. I have a modest collection from the Mediterranean and near East regions."

"I remember once seeing a photograph of your consulting room in Vienna. Greek and Roman busts, small artifacts displayed in glass cases. I seem to recall a large picture of the Egyptian temple at Abu Simbel, hanging on a wall above your infamous couch."

He laughed. "You have an excellent memory, the eye for detail, quite essential to someone of your profession. But I think you do not care much for what I call, the *Psychologie*, at least in the orderly universe you present to the reader."

"I give it little thought actually. People commit murder for very mundane reasons. Greed, lust, hatred, loyalty, or out of a sense of duty. Their motives are usually quite ordinary and straightforward. Nothing psychological about it, I'm afraid."

"Yet when it comes to your own life, I believe you spend much time looking inward. Introspection is the correct word in English, is it not?"

I saw him wince, the creases and lines of pain clearly visible around his mouth. He massaged his jaw with the fingers of his right hand as if this might erase his discomfort.

"You are ill. Why not take something for it?"

"I take nothing to dull the mind." He took a sip of his coffee then said, "This is only speculation, but I wonder if you became a writer in order to control your world, to influence what you could not in your own life."

"What do you mean?"

"That in your fictional creations, someone commits a crime, then is discovered after many red…what is *das* word?"

"Herrings," I supplied.

"*Ja,* red herrings, and then your criminal is punished. There is a certain kind of symmetry because you are in charge of your characters' destinies."

In some sense, he was right. My adult fairy tales, as I called them, had always felt safe. They revealed certain truths about human nature.

"Yet I believe if you look deeply into your stories, examine them closely, you will find yourself there, hidden among all the deceptions. Pardon me for saying this, but I think Agatha Christie may be your greatest mystery."

I could feel my anger rise. "What good is all this self-analysis anyway? My husband called it a sign of weakness. He'd tell me to ignore what I couldn't change and simply get on with life."

"May I call you by your first name?"

"What?" Then I thought, why not, now that, how did he put it, the ice is considerably broken. "Yes, of course you may."

"The best way to alleviate problems and to eliminate their symptoms is to talk about them. It is how we acquire self-knowledge. Do you not agree, Agatha?"

The noise from the engine subsided as the train began to slow its speed. I was aware of music in the background. Someone was playing a gramophone, a familiar Irving Berlin ballad I recognized as one of my husband's favorites, the tenor's voice urging me to remember:

"Remember the night
The night you said,
'I love you,'
Remember?"

During the past few years, I often felt as if I were outside my body observing this other woman playing a role in my life. If we couldn't understand ourselves, how could we ever hope to know others? I mulled this over before answering his question. "Yes, I suppose so." Sometimes one needed help, professional help that friends and relatives couldn't provide.

I picked up the silver teapot and freshened my cup, the lyrics of the song intruding again as I sat there quietly thinking of the man I had once loved, someone I had cared deeply about, had lived with for years and thought I had known. Until one night I discovered he wasn't that person at all.

The train gathered momentum, the rocking motion playing counterpoint to the lyrics:

"You promised that you'd forget me not
But you forgot to remember."

My hand began to shake. I put down the cup, managed to miss the saucer, and it tipped over staining the fine, white linen tablecloth. "But can we ever hope to understand ourselves completely?" I asked him. "Surely only God can know…"

"Should that stop us from searching, Agatha?"

I used my napkin to dab at the growing, brown spot that now covered considerable territory. "I really don't know."

"*Gut!* We are finally making some progress, *ja?*"

I suddenly felt like one of his patients, and I discovered I didn't like it one bit. I excused myself, and as I headed for the ladies lounge, the train made an abrupt turn, and I stumbled against the cocktail bar. I put out my hand and was able to stop from falling, but as I did this, I glanced back and it seemed everyone's eyes were upon me.

I pushed open the lounge door, the word "Ladies," etched on a brass plate, centered above a logo of twin lions proclaiming the train's royal lineage. After a few minutes to compose myself, I returned to the dining car. The waiter was clearing our table, and I was disappointed to find that the doctor had departed.

* * * *

I walked back to my compartment and found Dr. Freud sitting by the window reading his book, tilting it toward the light. He looked up and, with what I can only describe as genuine sincerity in his voice, said, "You have been very ill, Agatha. Would you like to tell me about it?" He leaned forward and motioned for me to sit across from him.

I wasn't sure what to do, but in the end, I did what he told me, and surrounded by the luxury appointments of gleaming wood and polished brass, the dam suddenly broke and my words rushed out so fast no power in Heaven or on earth could stop them.

"Some of my memories of those days seem clearer to me than others," I said, "but, still, I wonder if I remember events as they actually occurred or whether I only recall what people have told me."

"You must say what comes to your mind. Tell me what you think you remember." He reached over and held my hand, and, reassured by his strong, calming presence, I began.

"I knew for some time I had neglected my husband and daughter and had paid even less notice to the servants, to the planning of the meals, to the daily routine of running a large country house. My mother had recently passed away, you see, and I was on the verge of a nervous breakdown. I couldn't sleep. I couldn't think. I'd be writing a cheque to the butcher or grocer for some household expense and forget my name."

"You were in a deep state of melancholia," he told me. "You had no interest in the outside world. You had lost someone to whom you were greatly attached and with whom you identified closely."

"That's exactly how I felt."

"*Ja,* I understand. Please go on."

"I don't know that I can."

He told me to close my eyes.

I did as he suggested, shutting out everything in the coach, everything but his voice and the hypnotic, clickety-clack sound of the train steadily pushing forward over the steel rails, following its Alpine track.

"I remember an evening in early December. I was upstairs dressing for dinner. We were going abroad the next morning, a family outing, and I'd just finished packing away our things in two small cases."

I paused here, opened my eyes and saw Dr. Freud shaking his head, so I closed them again.

"My husband came through the bedroom door saying he hadn't bought the tickets, that we wouldn't be going on holiday. At first I thought it a good sign that he'd decided to spend the time at home with us. I started to tell him I was quite willing to change our plans, that our daughter would be so pleased, but he cut me off in mid-sentence."

This part was traumatic for me, and I had great difficulty telling it all to a stranger. What was I doing, sitting here verbalizing my most secret thoughts? My characters would never do this. No, they would evaluate the situation in the most practical manner then act accordingly with the help of whatever was at hand: a gun, a dagger, an undetectable poison, or a blunt instrument.

"My husband said he had found someone else." I opened

my eyes and looked out as we passed a peaceful village by a waterfall then watched the scene disappear around a bend as the train cleared the mountain pass and began to descend into the farm dotted highlands. "He said they were in love, and they meant to be together no matter the cost. Then he abruptly turned away from me and left the room."

"You must tell me everything you remember or think you remember about that night. Trust me. You will feel better afterwards."

"It is all so hazy. Time has made one day so much like the next."

"You must try, Agatha."

I closed my eyes. "I recall driving down a dark, country lane. I was running away, I suppose. People say, and I don't remember any of this, my Morris went off the road and into the tall grass. I must have hit my head hard against the dash or the steering wheel. I abandoned the car leaving my fur coat and dressing case behind."

"And then?"

"There was a grand hotel and a ballroom with a large, crystal chandelier. I remember dancing with a tall, well-dressed gentleman. We did a Charleston, I think, and then a tango followed by a waltz. I grew tired and rested my head on his shoulder…the rest is in bits and pieces."

"*Ja*, so?" He stroked his beard.

"I heard someone call me by a name I vaguely recognized. I looked up and a man grabbed my hand then pulled me across the dance floor and up the staircase to my room."

* * * *

The next morning I was travelling in a rather fancy limousine with this person who kept saying he was my husband, that we were going home, and, of course I knew in some part of my mind that he was my husband. But not for long. We divorced shortly afterwards, and he remarried." I stopped here for I had come to the end of what I remembered.

"Do you regret your marriage, Agatha?"

"As mad as it may seem, no. Not for a moment." My lack of hesitation surprised me.

"And over time you became yourself again, resumed your writing, and went on with your life."

"Yes, but there are still such gaps. I often wonder how many of my lost days have truly been accounted for and how many I have managed to piece together, construct from questionable sources? I wonder if I will ever know what really happened?"

"Does it matter?"

"I…I don't know," I said.

"For now, you must not worry too much. In time you may remember more. Perhaps there is a book or two in what you have told me. It will be good to finally write about it."

"But I couldn't. Not in my mysteries."

"No, I think you will not be so obvious. Maybe you will do so under another name."

"A pseudonym?"

"*Ja*, a false name. Writers can do that. It seems a bit deceitful, but it is…"

"Wonderful therapy?" I suggested.

"Exactly, once you get into the habit." Then he spoke slowly, while patting my hand. "I have a feeling, Agatha, for you the best is yet to come."

The engine drastically reduced speed, and as I looked out at the changing landscape, I realized we were approaching a major city.

"I must leave you now," he said, when the train came to a full stop at the Milan station.

I reached up to help him with his bags, and watched him rise slowly, the physical distress evident in his small, deliberate movements. He put on his hat and folded the heavy overcoat over his arm.

I thanked him. I wanted to let him know how grateful I was. For despite the unpleasantness of reliving the past, I discovered that I actually did feel better. I'd never spoken to anyone about that night except to the London psychiatrist; but at the time I was far too upset and intimidated to delve too deeply.

"You are most welcome, my dear," he said. "It was a pleasure to meet you." He put his arm around me and gave me a light hug.

"Please take care," I told him.

"I envy you," he said, with a wistful air. "How I wish I could continue on with you. In my earlier days…"

"Could you?"

"I am afraid that is not possible, but there is something I want you to remember. Will you do this for me?"

"Yes, of course, I will."

"You are not the simple, ordinary woman you show to the world, Agatha. You have great courage." He turned away from me, but before sliding open the coach door, he looked back, his eyes peering over the top of his spectacles, a warm affection in his smile. "I want you to know I have always preferred your books to those of Miss Sayers. *Wiedersehen.*" With that he waved goodbye and went down the corridor.

* * * *

The train was ahead of schedule when it pulled into the station at Stamboul. I put on my heavy woolen cloak to ward off the morning chill, and after I gathered up my few scattered belongs, I followed the porter off the train to collect my luggage.

Later by water taxi, I crossed the Bosporus, the narrow strip of water separating Europe from Asia. I glanced back and saw that the fog had begun to lift, the sun splashing its amber hues across the minarets and great dome of St. Sofia. The boat pushed on against the current, and I thought of my meeting with Dr. Freud, his words still clear in my mind:

"I have a feeling, Agatha, for you the best is yet to come."

I knew then I was ready for the next phase in my life, a second spring, so to speak, and armed with what I was sure the good doctor would call, my new self-knowledge, I decided to settle back and enjoy the ride.

◆◆◆

Paul Alan Fahey, Ed.D, created and edited *Mindprints*, an international literary journal for writers and artists with disabilities. During his tenure, *Mindprints* made "Writers Digest's Top 30 Short Story Markets" list for two consecutive years. His writing has appeared in *Byline*, *Kaleidoscope*, *The MacGuffin* and other literary journals and anthologies.

The Crime of Edward Palmer

Warren Bull

We shall be as a city upon a hill. The eyes of all people are upon us. – John Winthrop

"The devil is loose in Boston," said Edward Palmer. Thomas Dudley, recently elected Governor of the Massachusetts Bay Colony, and his closest supporters listened impassively. Dressed in black and looking down from their elevated chairs, they reminded Palmer of vultures waiting impatiently during the death throes of a stricken beast. Former Governor John Winthrop, who was still on the council, listened attentively. Other members of the council looked on with varying degrees of interest.

Palmer continued. "I beg your pardon for my rough, unlearned tongue." Even as he spoke, it occurred to him that these men would be slow and reluctant at forgiveness. Thomas Dudley had defeated John Winthrop for governor by haranguing about Winthrop's unwarranted leniency toward wrongdoers. Now the new governor and his supporters needed to demonstrate that they would swiftly and severely enforce the colony's rules—rules that were, after all, handed down by The Almighty, Himself. Palmer gathered his courage and resumed speaking.

"As God is my witness, I am certain you gentlemen have seen the signs. We call ourselves 'the people of God,' but it is clear that many among us have failed to keep Him in our thoughts. Many in Boston resist having to attend church twice a day. Many who do attend do not place their full attention on the excellent sermons. They fail to show fear of God, which is the foundation of all wisdom. There are other examples of sloth, disrespect and ungodliness that all of you know full well."

Palmer paused, wiped sweat from his brow and waited.

Dudley said, "Speak on."

"I have great respect for our former governor," said Palmer, nodding his head toward Winthrop. "But there are times when showing Christian love toward our brethren means that we must chastise our brothers and sisters in Christ to help them mend their ways and to move again toward redemption."

"Surely you don't mean that all will be saved," said Dudley, frowning.

"Oh, no sir," said Palmer. "Perish the thought. Men who are better educated and further along in biblical study than I am have explained to me that only the elect will go to heaven."

"Do you believe, then, that God's grace is all that is required for salvation?" asked Joseph Daniels, a Dudley supporter.

Palmer recognized the trap. He responded solemnly, "My betters tell me that grace alone will not suffice. They say it is the will of God that observance of the law and reverence for those who do God's work, such as those assembled here, are also required."

"It has come to my attention that you, yourself, have been charged with nearly falling asleep in church," retorted George Holloway, another council member.

"Sir, 'tis not so," said Palmer. "I admit that, on occasion, I close my eyes to concentrate on the words that are spoken."

Palmer bowed his head and remained silent for a moment. When he looked up again, Dudley spoke.

"Were you praying just now?"

"Yes, sir," answered Palmer. "I was thanking God for His grace toward my unworthy self."

Palmer did not reveal the rest of his thought, "...and for allowing me to sleep in church without snoring."

"Put your mind at ease, Mr. Palmer. While I am governor, there will be fewer mere brandings, nailing of ears, and scourging. I promise before God there will be more hangings. Firm chastisement will take the place of banishment and debate with those whose views diverge from the true path. I will not act like my esteemed predecessor. Now, why did you wish to address the council on these matters?"

"There is, sir, the matter of the iron frames—the ones that attach to the heels of those who have strayed from the light. Public display of sinners teaches others the dangers of sin. The frames served the city and colony well, but alas they are rusted beyond repair. Yet they are sorely needed now."

"We know that the billbowes are no longer serviceable," snapped Dudley. "But the council is not made of pounds and shillings. We must be prudent with every penny. Replacements from England would be excessively dear to buy and transport to our fair shores. Besides, there would be a long delay before they could be available."

"Indeed, sir," said Palmer. "I respectfully submit that there is an alternative, which is much less costly. It is more quickly and easily obtained and would serve just as well."

Council members whispered and muttered to each other.

"Perhaps you are not entirely wasting our time after all," said Dudley. "Speak now."

"There are contrivances known as stocks. They are made of wood. I have seen such devices in England. They securely and safely detain those whose behavior offends the law and the eye of God. I am, as you know, a humble carpenter. I believe I can construct stocks and transport them to the place set aside for public discipline, should it please the council."

"How long would it take and how much would it cost?" asked Dudley. He looked down his nose at Palmer who barely controlled a shiver.

"My deepest regret is that I cannot answer either question with complete assurance. Sir, I have never built stocks before. I only glanced at those I saw. I know that eventually I can construct them. But I may have to make several attempts. Certainly I will fail a number of times before I succeed. If I have the council's blessing and the promise of a fair wage for my labor, I will start at once."

"It sounds like a capital idea to me," said Dudley. He looked at the council. "Are there any dissenters? No? You may proceed."

Palmer bowed again and quickly left the chamber. He had expected to feel elated if his proposal succeeded, but all he felt was relief.

Two weeks later the council convened at the corner of King Street and Cornhill to view the stocks. Palmer explained the device with pride. "I was finally able to form this. It is made of solid oak so it will last a long time. It took many attempts and I put aside all other work, laboring day and night to build what you deserve. I am certain the council will be satisfied with it."

Palmer handed the bill for his labor and material to the new Governor who examined it with interest. Dudley folded it neatly and put it in his pocket.

"Can you show us how it works?" asked Dudley.

"Yes, sir," said Palmer. "The offender sits on the bench…"

"Show us, please," said Dudley with a rare smile.

"The offender sits here," said Palmer taking a seat on the bench. "He extends his legs forward until his ankles are in the half circles in the lower board." Palmer demonstrated.

"I imagine the pegs are removed from the frame so the upper board slides down," said Dudley, sliding the board into place as he spoke.

"Yes, sir," said Palmer. "You see how the upper half circle fits exactly with the lower. The wood is smooth. My ankles are not harmed in the least, but I cannot remove my legs from the stocks. Anyone with feet larger than a child's would be restrained. I can lean forward and touch it, but the upper board is much too heavy for me to lift from this position. The stocks can even be locked to prevent anyone who does not have authority from freeing the offender."

"Excellent," said Dudley. "I don't think we need to actually lock it. You won't be in it that long."

"No, sir," said Palmer with a weak smile.

Former governor Winthrop walked over to Palmer and gently placed his hand on Palmer's shoulder. Palmer looked up into his gentle eyes.

Dudley glared at Winthrop. Then he addressed Palmer. "This should serve for those who commit outrages. Speaking of which, why don't we discuss your shameless attempt at extortion by giving me a wantonly excessive bill for your services? Surely you don't think we would pay one pound, thirteen shillings and seven pence for a bench, a few boards and a frame?"

Palmer's voice caught in his throat.

"Were your labors worthy of Hercules?" asked Dudley. "Did they require the strength of Samson and leave you famished for the upcoming winter? With as much money as you dared to charge I could buy a gallon of oil, two bushels of peas and seventy-four pounds of bacon. Do you deny it?"

Palmer shook his head.

"I now call into session the court of the city of Boston of the Massachusetts Bay Colony with the governor, myself, as magistrate. What is your defense for this vile and ungodly behavior?"

Palmer sputtered.

"No defense? I thought not. There can be no justification for such conceit. I find you guilty of the crime of extortion and fine you five pounds. Also, I censure you and order you to sit in the stocks for the period of one hour. Has the convicted anything to say?"

Winthrop leaned over Palmer and warned him in a soft voice, "Consider the punishment for blasphemy before you respond."

Palmer clamped his mouth shut, shook his head and remained silent.

Dudley raised his eyebrows and waited expectantly. After a few moments he decided the man would remain mute. Dudley turned his back on Palmer and led the council members away.

Winthrop stayed behind long enough to murmur to Palmer, "Remember the scriptures, my friend: 'As ye sow, so shall ye reap.'"

♦ ♦ ♦

Warren Bull is an award-winning author with more than thirty published short stories. His novel *Abraham Lincoln for the Defense*, Publish America 2003 and Smashwords 2010, is available at http://www.smashwords.com/books/view/13700.

His short story collection *Murder Manhattan Style*, Ninth Month Publishing Co, 2010, is available at http://www.ninthmonthpublishing.com/books.html.

The Problem With Burlesque

Victoria Heckman

Violet Strange's heeled boots clicked dully on the sidewalk as she made her way, in the July heat, toward Nilbo's Theatre in New York City. Before she turned down the alley to the stage door, she paused to buy a paper from the corner newsie.

The headline caught her eye: FILM LAB STRIKE IMMINENT. Violet hadn't paid much attention to the conflict among the various aspects of film-making. The whole idea of movies was still so new—Violet had seen one brief but captivating clip of Isadora Duncan flailing her scarves as she danced around a garden—that the notion of organized labor and a strike in the industry, was rather unbelievable. This film thing was just a fad. It would never catch on.

Violet wrinkled her nose at the rotting-garbage smell of the alley. She opened the stage door. Sweat ran down her ribs, and she was relieved to step inside the murky, but relatively cool, backstage area. She inhaled deeply; the odd scents of cut lumber, old fabric, perfume—make-up perhaps? and fried onions made her tingle with excitement, as if she were going on stage, rather than just meeting with Horace Plith, manager of the Nilbo Theatre, a regular stop on the hot Vaudeville circuit. The Palace Performers, whose line up varied from town to town, and sometimes week to week, were a top-notch company, and made Nilbo's one of their longest stops. They had performed here for almost a month, with another two weeks on the contract. Mr. Plith had contacted Violet because of increasingly violent sabotage.

Violet Strange, a lovely young woman who occasionally assisted a private detective firm, was the perfect undercover operator for this job. In 1921, proper ladies did not engage in such work, but Violet had a natural talent for ferreting out the truth.

With her clear, guileless eyes, shining hair, and chameleon personality, Violet could fit in anywhere. Her brains and etiquette succeeded where brawn might fail.

Violet carefully stepped over ropes and cables, seeking Mr. Plith's office in the maze of curtains, set pieces and props. The ceiling stretched high above, a mare's nest of pulleys and curtains suspended from the roof joists. She made out the long shadow of an iron catwalk, access to the hundreds of stage lights mounted nearby.

A small sign reading *Office & Dressing Rooms* with a downward arrow indicated a wooden staircase. She descended carefully, holding her skirt tight against her. The steps creaked alarmingly, and in the dim, yellow light she intently watched her feet.

At the bottom, she smacked into a solid body and gasped in alarm, stepping back. Her small reticule and newspaper fell and she sat down hard on the steps, heart pounding.

The figure was in shadow, backlit by light spilling from an open door. "Miss Strange?" He extended a hand and Violet breathed again.

"Mr. Plith?" She rose, ignoring the proffered hand, brushed off her skirt, and retrieved her purse and newspaper.

"Yes. I'm sorry I startled you. Are you all right?"

"Yes, thank you." Mr. Plith remained quite close. "Shall we go into your office?"

"Of course."

He led her to a small, cramped office. Floor to ceiling shelves lined three walls, stuffed with scripts and theatre-related material. A small, ratty settee crouched in a corner, and an overflowing desk blocked the opposite wall.

Mr. Plith indicated the rickety chair fronting the desk. Violet sat and he took up his post behind it. Violet glanced around, noting details. A bust of Shakespeare wore a small fedora, and had penciled-on long, curling mustaches and a black eye. This evidence of humor reassured Violet. The room itself, while confining, was snug and cozy with its crowded shelves and the lingering odors of pipe tobacco and coffee.

She took note pad and pen from her purse and assessed Mr. Plith as he cleared a space on the desk in front of him, and rummaged through a stack of papers. "Just a moment. I had it right here," he said.

He was shorter than she had realized while she sat on the stairs, and was beginning to lose his hair. She estimated his age at thirty. No wedding ring. His spectacles slid down his nose as he searched, and he pushed them up quickly.

His white shirt was unbuttoned at the collar, and he wore no tie. The cuffs were turned up, stained and frayed at the edges. He wore a snugly buttoned vest that looked like Violet's bodice felt: too hot and too tight. Sweat stains ringed his armpits and glowing beads dotted his face.

"Ah, ha!" He held a sheet aloft. A stack of reviews cascaded gently to the floor. "Thank you so much for coming, Miss Strange. As I said in my letter to your employers, our theatre is under some kind of attack. For weeks, one thing after another has occurred to set us back."

"Please describe these events." Violet sat with pen poised.

"At first, it was small things. You know, a costume piece moved. A prop missing, and turning up later in a strange place. A costume slashed. A kleig light fell from the ceiling rack one night after the show. Things got worse and worse. Then two days ago, Miss Apples, our star, was locked in her dressing room."

"She locked herself in?"

"No. She was locked in from the outside. We finally called Ed, our set builder, to come and take off the door or drill out the knob or something. By the time he got there with the tools, Miss Apples was hysterical. She screamed and cried and threw herself against the door, and when she rattled the knob again, it just opened."

"It 'just opened?'" Violet had been writing all of this down. "Who was outside her door while all this was going on?"

"I don't know. I sent a stage hand to get Ed, but everyone was running around, calling through the door to Lotta—that's Miss Apples."

"Where is Miss Apples' dressing room?"

"The last one down the hall. Hers is the largest private dressing room. Would you like to see it?"

"Yes, but not just yet. Please go on with the incidents. What else happened?"

"The cast and crew started to grumble about ghosts and some said the theatre is haunted."

"Haunted?"

"Well, practically every theatre in the world is supposed to be haunted, but I have to admit," he ran a hand through his thinning hair, "we've never had things disappear so frequently, or doors locked like that before. I don't believe it's a ghost. I almost wish it were. I'm sure someone's behind this, but I don't know who or why."

"Perhaps a practical joke? They are not unheard of in the theatre, yes?"

"If so, no one's owned up, and it's getting out of hand." Mr. Plith pushed his glasses up and massaged the bridge of his nose. "No, I don't think that's it."

"Have you called the police?"

"Yes. We had a crew meeting about the problems. Afterward, they not only continued, but they got worse. Things were damaged or stolen. A number of missing props and costumes are still missing. And now this with Miss Apples."

"Did you report this latest incident?"

"Of course. It was the only way to get Miss Apples calm

enough to perform. She insisted on a body guard, too." He sighed heavily. "I haven't arranged that yet, but she's our main attraction; I have to keep her happy."

"So why have you called me in?"

"The police say they can't help. There's no real evidence. I must admit, everything is so easily explained away. I need to know what's going on. If the theatre loses the top acts, or if the rumor gets out that Nilbo's is haunted, we'll lose money. My job is at stake here, Miss Strange. The police say they can't help unless they have some clues. I'm here eighteen hours a day and I have no clues. I need some help. I'm paying you out of my own pocket, Miss Strange. I'm desperate. I need my job. I love my job." He shoved up his glasses again and sniffed.

Violet wondered if he'd been an actor. "Why would someone want to harm the company?"

"Believe me, I have no idea. The company books new talent all the time, but the headliners usually stay for a while. Maybe someone has a grudge against one of them? Something personal?"

"Do you have any evidence of that?"

"No. I'm just guessing." He sighed again. "We all need our jobs. We are in show business because we love it. Because we can't *not* do it." His eyes, magnified behind his glasses, trapped hers. "The theatre is a very incestuous business, Miss Strange." At her raised eyebrows he stammered out an apology. "I just mean, we travel together, perform together. It forms bonds, relationships. Those relationships are subject to a great deal of strain, especially when something like this happens." His face was crimson.

"I see. You say the sabotage began small, with things, and now has moved on to a member of the company?"

"That's correct. I don't want to tell the performers, but I'm worried. What if something worse happens?"

"I'll do my best to find out what's going on, Mr. Plith. I

will ask two things of you, for now." Violet stood. "First, that you grant me complete access to everything in this building; the backstage areas, dressing rooms, the house, and even your office." Mr. Plith licked his lips and nodded. "Second, you must tell no one who I am, and why I'm here. That includes your actors and crew, even the owner of the theatre."

"But, Mr. Nilbo should know, shouldn't he? He owns the building. And I don't know how long I can keep this from Mr. Schilling. Oh, God, what a mess."

"Who's Mr. Schilling?"

"He's the booking agent."

"What exactly is a booking agent?"

"He books all the acts on the circuit. If he doesn't like you, you're in big trouble. A booking agent can get you great acts, or you can end up with freak shows."

"I see."

"No, really. He also holds the performers in the palm of his hand. If a booking agent doesn't like an act, it ends up on the 'Death Trail.'"

"'Death Trail?'"

"Small venues, no money, no future. I tell you, Miss Strange, this is a harsh business. You have to want it more than anything."

"All right, Mr. Plith. I understand, but I repeat, no one can know who I am, or I can't do my job and I won't assist you. You and I, Mr. Plith, are the only ones who are to know. Are we agreed?"

Mr. Plith sighed piteously. "I just feel so alone in this. It would help to have someone to talk to." He poked his glasses up.

"Mr. Plith." Violet held out her hand. "You have me."

Horace Plith stood and shook Violet's hand over the desk. "You're right, Miss Strange. I have you. I feel a little better already. Have you given any thought to what your role here will be?"

"My role?" Panic flared in Violet's stomach. "I'm not a performer."

"Of course not!" Mr. Plith, as the theatre manager, looked shocked at the prospect of Violet on stage. "I simply meant, what will you do to explain your presence?"

"Oh. Yes. I will be your personal assistant."

"But I've never had a personal assistant. Won't that be suspicious?"

Violet eyed him: Unclean, rumpled attire, tousled hair, smudged glasses, his figure slack and dejected. His office looked like the result of an explosion in a paper factory. She had never met anyone who appeared more in need of a personal assistant.

"I think the company will believe me. Now, let's go look at that dressing room."

Violet examined Miss Apples' dressing room and found nothing unusual except that a second exit door had been nailed shut and appeared to be unused. She inspected the other dressing rooms, climbed the catwalk, roamed the halls, and then sat in the darkened house. A work light on stage dimly illuminated the vast space, and the gilt-edged procenium glowed. She pondered the events Mr. Plith had recounted, occasionally referring to her notebook, tilting it toward the stage in the gloom. She felt the ambiance shift—a heightening of activity, an increased hum of energy, before she actually heard or saw anything. She held her breath in anticipation.

A door opened and a rush of sound poured through the building as the actors arrived for the first show of their "two a day." Bawdy laughter, and ribald comments punctuated the general chatter as the company surged, ebbed and flowed around the costume racks and prop tables. Violet saw a pattern in their seemingly random flitting. Without conscious effort, they checked their costumes and props, a well-worn routine upon entry to the theatre. From her vantage point, she could not see into the wings, but the main curtains had been pulled back and the narrower "blacks" behind them were raised, allowing Violet a better view than the audience would have during performance. Once the costume/prop check had been completed, the performers noisily trooped downstairs to the dressing rooms.

Mr. Plith had said most of the company used two large dressing rooms, one for the men, and one for the women. Several specialty acts or headliners had private dressing rooms. He added that private dressing space was always at a premium, and cause for dispute among the company. At present, Miss Apples had the number one dressing room, and the other main act occupied number two. During a previous run, the main acts had fought so viciously over the private rooms that he had placed paint buckets and drop cloths in front of the locked doors, saying they were being redecorated and were unavailable.

Violet decided it was time to begin her own 'act' as Mr. Plith's personal assistant. She left the house through a side door and followed the sloping hallway to the backstage entrance.

The rumble of voices grew louder as she descended to the lower level. She peered into Mr. Plith's office, hoping he would introduce her to the members of the troupe. No luck. She entered the women's dressing room. Bare, bright light bulbs fringed a row of mirrors along one wall, bringing the room into sharp focus. A long dressing table fronted the mirrors, its surface lost under a sea of feathers, jewelry, make-up, programs, and implements Violet could only assume were tools of the trade.

Violet approached a young woman who was applying stage make-up with a lavish hand. Violet had never seen performers close up, and was slightly alarmed at the garish appearance of red-apple cheeks, blue eyelids, and glistening ruby lips. The woman's eyes had a startled, lop-sided appearance as she wrestled to apply a feathery false eyelash.

"Hello," Violet began.

"Hold this," the woman commanded, placing Violet's fingers over a set of tweezers holding the lash set in place.

Violet held her breath, afraid she might jab the tweezers into the woman's eye. The woman showed not the slightest concern, as she poked, rather roughly, at the other end of the lash piece.

"Thanks," the woman said. "You can let go, now." Violet set down the tweezers with a rush of breath. "Are you new?"

"Yes. I'm Violet."

"Great. What's your act? Biff said we were getting some new girls. You the one who does that tassel thing?"

"Tassel thing?"

"You sure got the bod for it," the woman continued, eyeing Violet's trim figure and clear skin.

Violet blushed. "No. I'm not a performer. I'm Mr. Plith's new personal assistant."

"Biff's got himself a nice one, huh?" The woman examined herself in the mirror, evidently satisfied.

"Biff?"

"That's what we call ol' Plith. Behind his back, a'course."

Violet tilted her head politely. She had often found that silence elicited more response than direct inquiry.

"You know, he's such a milque-toast, and it's kind of a football, manly sort of nick-name. It fits, in an opposite way." She looked at Violet quizzically in the mirror, as though she had disparaged the theatre manager to a person who *mattered.* "I mean, it's all in fun, you know."

"Oh, yes," said Violet. "What is your name, and what is your act?"

"I'm Ruby, and I do a song and dance number and a sketch with my partner, Timmy Timmons. We're Timmons and Hart," she finished proudly.

"Nice to make your acquaintance. I'd like to meet everyone, but there are so many." Violet looked around the room in dismay at more than a dozen women, in various stages of undress and make-up. The company would leave New York in two weeks, and the sheer number of suspects was daunting. She hadn't met the men yet, or the performers in private dressing rooms.

"I can help you out, there," said Ruby. She stood and hollered, "Hey! Hey, everybody!" The voices subsided. "This is Violet, Biff's new personal assistant. She has a lot to catch up on, and we all wanna help her out, right?" Silence. "Right?" Some mumbled agreement. "So, take a minute to say hello and tell her your act. Besides, we want to make a good impression before she's thrown to the wolves!" The room erupted into laughter.

"What do you mean?" Violet asked.

"Just wait 'til you meet the men—you might want some friends in this dressing room!"

"Aren't some of them married? Or with girlfriends?"

"Sure they are. Since when does that have anything to do with it? Button me." Ruby slipped into a brightly colored dress with a full skirt and a white bib.

Violet buttoned, her mind awhirl. She thought of her own dear husband Roger, then firmly pushed him from her mind. She needed to concentrate on her job. Get it finished and return to her sane, normal world. She moved about the room, learned names and acts, and excused herself with a sigh. She was not up to greeting the men, if the women were this forward. She decided to try the headliners next.

Her hand was raised to knock on Miss Apples' door when a scream rang out from inside. She threw the door open. An attractive, scantily clad, heavily made up woman held out a swatch of fabric and screamed.

As Violet stepped forward, someone pushed her violently. She crashed into the woman and they reeled onto a pink velvet settee. The screams turned to indignant shrieks.

"You stupid cow! What the hell do you think you're doing?"

Violet opened her mouth to apologize and heard Mr. Plith say, "I'm so sorry, Miss Apples. Mr. Nilbo and I were meeting in my office when we heard you, uh, call, and in my haste to come to your aid, I tripped over the threshold and fell into Miss Violet, here."

Violet recognized the man with Mr. Plith. When she took this case, Violet did a hasty bit of research on the legendary E.F. Nilbo. He had built theatre after theatre in New York, Boston, and Atlantic City. His venues were known for their lavish lobbies, marble floors, green rooms, and gold fixtures in the lounges. His long reach now controlled nearly 100,000 people in this business.

"Who cares?" Miss Apples immediately changed her attention and her attitude. "Why, Mr. Nilbo! Such a pleasure to see you. And how have you been?" She rose and rearranged her wisp of a garment, to no noticeable increase in coverage.

"Just fine, Lotta. And you?" Mr. Nilbo's large, richly clad frame diminished that of Horace Plith. Mr. Nilbo smelled strongly of tobacco and his booming voice filled the small space. Violet resisted the impolite urge to cover her ears with her hands.

"Who have we here?" His shiny, greased hair reflected the mirror lights as he bent to inspect her.

"I'm Miss Violet." She put out her hand. He captured her delicate fingers with his meaty hand, raising them to his moist lips.

A gallant, old-world gesture, but Violet felt only revulsion as the lips slid toward her wrist. She fluttered her eyelids and freed her hand. He stared at her, and she forced herself not to wipe her hand on her skirt.

"Oh, Mr. Nilbo! It's just such an honor to meet you! I've heard so much about you," she gushed. "I am just the luckiest girl in the world. My first day here in the exciting world of show business, and I meet you, of all people!"

"Yes, my dear. Are you an actress?" She shook her head. "Dancer?" He eyed her figure rather longer than was polite.

"Oh, no! I'm not anything at all."

"Oh, come now. With your looks and presence. . .surely, you sing like a bird?"

"Mr. Nilbo," she giggled. "I'm not a performer! I could never. . ." she let the sentence hang, hoping to imply she could never aspire to such a lofty goal. In reality, the idea of going on stage made her feel nauseated.

"Well. We shall talk about his more, later. Privately."

To Violet's relief, Lotta Apples didn't care for second billing in the little dressing room drama. "Miss Violet. How nice to meet you." Her lip curled slightly. "You can be my dresser. That is, if you're *really* not a performer?"

"Yes, Miss Apples. Anything I can do to help." Violet was pleased by this development, since Lotta Apples seemed to be the current center of the sabotage. It also wouldn't hurt to connect to Mr. Nilbo through Lotta, and avoid being alone with him. She hoped.

"So, my dear, what was all the commotion about?" Mr. Nilbo stroked Lotta's arm.

Lotta looked momentarily blank. "My costume! Someone slashed it!" She thrust out a piece of pale blue, sheer fabric that would not make an adequate hat veil.

"My goodness! There's hardly any left!" Violet said.

"What?" Lotta used both hands to display the piece. "It's all here, it just has this hole in it. I can't use it now! And it's my new one!"

A long rent crossed several seams through the main part of the garment.

"Where was the costume the last time you saw it intact?" Violet asked.

"It was on my rack here, with all the rest."

"And this was the only piece damaged?"

"I don't really know. I was going to wear this one, so I saw it."

"Why don't you check?" Violet caught Horace Plith's eye and he frowned at her, shaking his head slightly. She raised her eyebrows in inquiry.

Lotta helped clarify his warning. "Well, look who's awfully nosy, miss." She folded her arms and stared at Violet. Mr. Nilbo also eyed her strangely.

"Oh, Miss Apples, I didn't mean to be. It's just that, if I'm to be your dresser, I have to understand your costumes, don't I? I wouldn't want to make a mistake. After all, you are a *star*!" This breathless declaration seemed to mollify all three of them.

Horace blew out a breath. "Well, Mr. Nilbo, things seem under control here, for the moment. Why don't you and I continue our discussion in my office?"

The big man grunted in assent, but his gaze lingered on Violet as the men walked out.

Violet heard Horace greet someone in the hall. "Schilling! What are you doing here?" The voices faded as they continued toward the office.

"Schilling, you jerk," Lotta mumbled.

"Miss Apples? Is something wrong?"

"I just hate that man."

"Who?"

"That smarmy booking agent."

"What did he do?"

"You name it." Lotta poked furiously at her costumes. "He books the acts on this circuit. He used to be a little nobody booking 'The Death Circuit—'"

"The Death Circuit?"

"Oh, you know. The little clubs with horrible hotels, no pay and roaches you could saddle up. Somehow though, Schilling suddenly jumped to the big time."

"What happened?"

"I don't know." Lotta fingered the torn cloth. "I guess that's strange. In this business, gossip falls like rain and I haven't heard how he made the jump. I do know it's unusual—once small time, always small time; once an opening act, always an opening act. I was a child star, you know."

"No, I didn't know." Violet took the costume.

"Yeah, well. Back then, Schilling wanted to handle me personally. Fortunately, although I was green, I wasn't stupid. I said no. Now I'm a headliner, and look who's right on my tail. In more ways than one." She raised her eyebrows and laughed.

Violet absorbed this information, but thought it prudent to return to her role as 'dresser.' "Miss Apples, I don't sew, and your costume looks unusable."

"You got that right." Lotta grabbed the costume and threw it on the settee in disgust. "Cost me a mint. Now I gotta go with one of the old ones." Lotta rifled through the bright garments on the racks.

To Violet's untrained eye, they looked beautiful, flimsy, and insubstantial, but most importantly, unharmed. "Are they all right?" she asked.

"All right? They stink! I've got nothing to wear!"

"I mean, are they whole? Undamaged?"

"Yeah." Lotta sat at her dressing table and began to apply more make-up. "Find me that green one with the leaves."

Violet located the garment and laid it on the settee.

"Help me change."

Violet looked at the costume, at a complete loss as to how to assist. "Since it's my first time, perhaps you could tell me how best to. . ."

"Sure, kid. First is the nude bodysuit." Violet never said the word 'nude,' and rarely heard it except as a reference to art. She controlled her discomfort and helped Lotta into an ankle to collar bone, flesh colored, skin tight body suit. Once encased, Lotta was quite covered, although to the audience, she would appear, well, nude. Then Violet wound, draped, pinned and tied on a series of leaves and vines, covering Lotta in layers of foliage. Last, she was directed to attach papier mache 'apples' at strategic points.

A sharp knock at the door and the call, "Ten minutes, Miss Apples."

"Yeah, yeah." Miss Apples rearranged her stiff, unmoving hair to her satisfaction. Violet could only watch in awe.

Another knock. "You're on in five, Miss Apples."

"I'm coming, for Pete's sake." Lotta surveyed herself in the mirror once more.

"Miss Apples? What is it, exactly, that you do?"

"I'm only the best burlesque act on the circuit. You watch me and you watch a star. Come on. Get an eye full." She propelled a slightly stunned Violet out the door, causing another collision, this time with the stage manager. He called, "Places."

"On my way, Stanley. On my way." Lotta stationed Violet in the wings saying, "We wait here until I go on."

Violet was completely mesmerized by the orchestra and the tumblers and jugglers on stage. "When do you go on?"

"After this comic. He's pretty good. When he's sober."

"How many acts are there?"

"Thirty-five."

Thirty-five acts was a lot of suspects. Then throw in Mr. Plith, Mr. Nilbo, Stanley, the stage crew, the mysterious Schilling, and she was looking at insurmountable odds. Violet felt her first twinge of doubt.

The music changed. A lot. No longer fun-filled and campy, lyrical or dramatic—it was lusty. Definitely lusty. Music to shake and wiggle to. Lotta grabbed her hand and pulled her to the edge of the blacks behind the main curtain.

"Stay here," Lotta commanded. "Watch and learn." She circled the blacks and disappeared. The stage went dark, an inch at a time. The audience began to hoot and holler raucously. The music faded away. Then in a blaze of light and a blare of horns, the stage was bright and filled with. . . an apple tree. The sensuous music built and the tree rolled smoothly downstage. Just past center, the tree stopped its forward movement, and its branches began to writhe. Piece by piece, the limbs drooped and fell, until a feminine form emerged. The tree trunk held Lotta's body, with her arms amid the twigs and leaves. She stepped out of the tree and sinuously wrapped herself around the bole. She played peekaboo, she unwrapped vines from herself, she threw apples and kisses to the audience. At one point she plucked a large 'apple' from the tree and rolled on it up and down the stage; rolled it up and down her body, front to back as if it was attached by magic. Violet was as enchanted as the audience.

With a crash from the orchestra, Lotta finished and disappeared into her tree trunk. The stage went black. A moment later, Lotta was at Violet's side, breathless and glowing. "Come on, Violet. I have to get out of this costume. I'm dying of the heat." She charged off in the dark toward the dressing room stairs, calling over her shoulder, "Bring me a drink."

Violet hadn't even had time to tell her how wonderful she'd been. She set off in search of a glass of water.

When Violet returned to the dressing room, Lotta was creaming off her makeup. "At last! What took you so long? Stanley usually has it ready for me." She took a big swig and choked, spitting water all over the floor. "What the hell is this?"

"Water?"

"I can tell that. What happened to the *gin*?"

"I'm sorry, Miss Apples. I didn't know. I'll be right back." No wonder Stanley waved and tried to get her attention. Well, now she knew. She found the glass on his podium and brought it back to the dressing room. Lotta drank deeply.

"That's better. Now help me off with this damn thing and rinse it out so I can wear it for tonight's show. I'm going to have a little nap now. You go 'way. I'm tired." Lotta lay back on the settee and immediately began to snore. Violet did as directed, then quietly put the "Do Not Disturb" sign on the door and went out. She had so little time! She still hadn't met the men. Thirty-five acts! She refused to think about it. One act at a time, she thought, and marched toward the men's dressing room.

Her knock went unanswered, but the chaos she heard inside made her unwilling to open the door on a roomful of men in various stages of undress. She would wait until they came out for their acts and talk to them one at a time. Perhaps she could talk to the stage crew before they took their dinner break between shows. She mounted the stairs, noticing the shift in energy in the theatre. While she had attended Lotta, the show had ended and the audience had departed. Work lights lit the stage and the crew moved freely about. She ducked behind the black curtain that covered the entire back wall of the stage, allowing performers to cross from one side to another, unseen by the audience. As she passed the spiral iron stairs to the catwalk, she heard whispers. She froze in the folds of the black curtain.

"What did you come here for, you idiot?"

"You didn't call me."

"Sheesh. I said you'll get your money."

"Yeah? I'd better. I took care of it. I been taking care of things for you."

"It's done?"

"Yes. That's what you're paying me for, isn't it?"

"Remember what I said, nothing permanent."

"I said, *it's done*."

"You're a pain in my side and I can't wait 'til I don't see

your stupid face anymore. This whole thing's gonna change, and I'm gonna be at the top of the new heap, just like I'm at the top of this one. They're gonna talk, I tell you, and then you'll really see something."

"Just keep making it worth my while to cooperate, and you won't have to see my 'stupid face.' We'll both be rich and free."

Violet heard feet descending the iron stairs. She wanted to see the speakers, but not to be caught eavesdropping. She dashed down the stairs to the dressing areas, hoping the fluttering blacks and busy workers had hidden her. She counted to ten, then returned to the stage manager's podium.

Horace stood there with Stanley and a man she didn't recognize. They abruptly stopped talking as she approached.

"Hello, Violet. How are things going with your first show?" Horace asked.

"Oh, fine, thank you, Mr. Plith."

"I don't believe we've met," the stranger said smoothly. "I'm William Schilling, booking agent for the best acts in Vaudeville. And you are?"

"I'm Violet. Miss Apples' new dresser."

"How lovely. She's a lucky woman." He smiled, showing a great many large teeth. His hair oil smelled strong and perfume-y. Almost feminine. "Too bad you're not a performer. I could get you on the top, too."

Violet shuddered inside, but gave him a charming smile. "I'm sure you could, Mr. Schilling, but I really love my work." That wasn't a lie. She was determined to discover who threatened this special world of ego and sensitivity known as theatre. In less than a day, she had seen magic created on that stage. The dedication and sacrifice the performers and crew displayed, all for love of the art, made her furious that someone would try to take it away.

"Stanley, could I have a word later?" Violet asked.

Stanley looked startled. "Sure, Miss Violet. I guess so. About what?" All three men looked at her inquiringly.

She thought quickly. "Just something for Miss Apples. No rush. Thank you, Stanley. If you'll excuse me, I'm sure you men have important things to discuss." She turned to go and noticed the newspaper tucked under Mr. Schilling's arm. Its blaring headline connected with an audible 'click' in her brain. Violet hurried back to Lotta's dressing room, where she'd left her own newspaper and purse.

Lotta still snored on the settee. Violet sat at the dressing table and read the front page article on the film lab strike. Apparently, the film industry was more formidable than Violet had realized. Not only in New York and New Jersey, a parallel movement in California had reached unheard-of popularity. Some sort of alliance was trying to unite all aspects of the film production industry in a single union, from camera operators and film labs, all the way to the projection booth. At the end of the article, the paper referred her to a related, smaller article inside, where she confirmed the motive for the sabotage, and where she found her main suspect. Now to set the trap.

Violet contemplated all she'd heard and seen the last few hours. She drafted two similar messages and had a boy deliver them before the second show.

Lotta still hadn't moved. That seemed odd. Even in sleep, one turned, shifted, didn't one? Violet checked her watch and saw that the call time for the company was upon them. She gently shook the star's arm.

"Lotta? Time to get up. Get ready for your show." Lotta didn't move. Her arm lay slack on the settee. Although somewhat reassured by her loud snoring, Violet searched out Horace Plith.

Horace followed her back to the dressing room. "I saw this once, in another company. You say you gave her the glass of gin and she just passed out?" Violet nodded. "She always has a glass of gin. Something else was in that gin. Cripes. She could be out for hours. What are we gonna do?"

"She'll be all right, won't she?" Why wasn't Horace more concerned for Lotta's well-being?

"Fine, fine." He paced distractedly. "This is just one more thing."

"You mean this is sabotage, too? She didn't just over indulge?"

"No, no. Lotta can drink a sailor under the table. This is deliberate, to keep her from performing." He checked his watch. "She goes on in an hour. She'll never recover in time. If we don't have the burlesque star, we're in trouble. People come here just for that. We're gonna lose contracts, artists, bookings, the whole thing could fail and I'd be held responsible! I'd never get another job in Vaudeville again!"

"Now calm down, Mr. Plith. You won't be held accountable, I'll see to that. I think I've found out what's going on, and you're right. It's been deliberate, just as you've said, and for the reason you just stated."

"What? To run me out of Vaudeville?"

"No, Mr. Plith. You are distraught. A much bigger picture is at stake here, and I do mean picture. Rest assured, the show will go on in an hour, but first I have to do some things. You do your job, and I'll do mine, and I think we'll both be through with our business by closing tonight."

Mr. Plith, rumpled and dejected, sighed. "Yes, Miss Strange. What should I do now?"

"Your job, Mr. Plith. Just do your job, but stay out of your office. I'm going to need it. Miss Apples will be fine here." Violet swept from the room and up the stairs to the back door. Leary, another operative from her agency, had received her message and come to assist her with her own little drama. She quickly explained what she wanted. He nodded and moved off into the dark.

She hurried to Horace's office and crouched, well-hidden, behind the settee in the corner. After several minutes in the dark, she heard the voices she'd been waiting for.

"What do you mean, sending me that message?"

"I sent you? You sent me!"

"Look, I'm paying you to do a job. If you won't be so damn greedy for five minutes, we'll both be rich. I told you, this kind of thing takes time, but the payoff will be huge."

"I know. I said I'd wait. What do you mean by threatening to expose me? There's no proof. Besides, it was your idea."

"No, but I do have proof you drugged Miss Apples."

"What? You *told* me to! I'll take you down with me. You said make sure she can't perform. I did. I've been leaking information on the circuit for weeks about how your theatre is wracked with problems. I'm having trouble booking the good acts already. What are you talking about, me rushing things?"

"Look, Schilling, I wouldn't give you the time of day if you hadn't made it impossible to ignore you. I brought you up from the small time to the big time circuit, but that wasn't good enough for you."

"Your generosity is overwhelming. You're planning to dump all the people who made you what you are today—rich, famous, powerful. And for what? More money. Maybe you're right, movies are getting big. But they'll never replace Vaudeville. Never. You're naive to think people will want to sit in a theatre and watch moving pictures when they could watch something real."

"You're the one who's naive and greedy, and it's going to get you killed."

"Are you threatening me?"

"You just watch your step. When this whole thing's over and my theatre's making money hand over fist from movies. . . think of it—no actors to pay, no overhead, no contract disputes—

you'll still be peddling your 'stars,' and then where will you be? Some little nothing hall with a tabloid musical and a monkey act."

Violet rose, somewhat painfully, from behind the settee. "Well, gentlemen, I see I was right. You are a despicable scoundrel," she pointed to Nilbo, "to displace all the actors who have made you what you are. To turn this gorgeous place into some kind of *movie house!*" She sounded as if she meant brothel. "And to think, the public knows nothing about how you trod upon people to get to your precious perch at the top."

"You," she turned to Schilling. "You are just as bad. Exploiting your acts, your performers, then blackmailing your way into an even more influential position. You both should be ashamed of yourselves."

Nilbo glanced at Schilling. "Take care of her. I'm not letting some little missy spout off and ruin months of planning. We still have this show to finish, and I think a number of people will cancel and I'll really be on my way. With no burlesque act, and my last little surprise, we'll be right on schedule."

"What little surprise?" Schilling asked. "You didn't tell me about anything else."

"That's why it's a surprise. Now get moving. She's a liability, and I have work to do." Nilbo sat at the desk and began to go through the drawers.

"You are making a serious mistake, sir," Violet began.

"Shut her up." Nilbo didn't look up. Schilling grabbed Violet's arm and dragged her over the settee.

As she opened her mouth to scream Schilling said, "No one can hear you down here, and you're just going to make me mad. You don't want to make me mad, do you?"

Violet saw his overlarge teeth in a feral grin as his fingers bit into her arm and thought better of screaming. For now. She slumped meekly and he pushed her out the door, shutting it behind them. The empty hallway echoed with the performance above, and in the dim light, she saw no sign of her co-agent.

Schilling shoved her into Lotta's dressing room and she felt a momentary lift, knowing that would be one of the first places searched. He went to the second door, released a hidden catch and opened it, revealing a short hallway and a flight of stairs, a closed door at the top. The hallway held the slumped, inert figure of Leary, her 'muscle.' Schilling bound her arms and mouth tightly saying, "I'll finish you later. I have work to do." He slammed the door, leaving her in darkness.

She listened for Leary's breathing. He was alive. Her brain whirled furiously. She turned her back and felt along the door with her bound hands. She carefully mounted the short stairs and felt for the upper door. A locked knob. She groaned in frustration and started to sit on the top step. Her heel caught in her long skirt and she lost her balance, falling awkwardly down the steps onto Leary's body. Her pain was diminished by something she discovered on the way down. A trickle of blood seeped down her wrists—she had hit something sharp. She felt carefully along the stair wall, ignoring her throbbing head. A nail. She turned her back and began to poke and saw her bonds against the protrusion. She had no idea how much time passed until she was free—arms aching, head pounding—but free.

Once again, she felt along the sealed door. A voice she heard from the other side gave her hope. Horace Plith was trying to rouse Lotta.

"Horace! Mr. Plith! Help!" Violet yelled. Silence from the other side.

"Miss Violet?"

"Yes! It's me! Help me, let me out!"

"Where are you?"

"Behind the nailed-shut door! Hurry, I must get out!"

"But I don't see how. . . "

"Feel for a catch, a hole, something near the knob, I think."

"I've got it!" The door swung open.

"Hurry, help me. We've got to save this show!" Violet saw Lotta still sprawled on the settee. She grabbed the body suit and the apples. Horace stared, open-mouthed.

"Who's that?"

"Who?" Violet kicked off her shoes and struggled to pull up the body stocking under her dress.

"Lying in there."

"Oh! My goodness, I almost forgot! That's Mr. Leary. From my agency. I called him in, but they got to him first. He's alive. Close your eyes," she commanded. He did and she wriggled out of her dress and into the rest of the body suit. "Help me, now." She directed a completely stunned Horace into assisting her into the intricate weavings of vines and fruit. A knock rang out.

"Miss Apples, you're on in ten!"

"Thank you," Violet called. She quickly applied make-up and arranged her hair.

"What do you think you're doing?" said Horace.

"I am going on for Miss Apples. Don't you see? If I don't, and there is no burlesque act, Nilbo and Schilling's plan takes another step forward. Maybe an irrevocable step."

"What are you talking about?"

"I don't have time to explain. See if you can get Mr. Leary awake. He knows what to do. If not, we'll just have to improvise." Horace nodded.

"I'm awake," came from the hidden hallway. Leary leaned against the door frame, rubbing his head. "Violet? Is that you?"

"Yes. It's an emergency. The plan is still on. Wait where I told you. You are all right, aren't you?"

"Yeah, sure. I've had worse heads than this after a night with the boys in McGinty's."

"Fine. I'll see you later. Horace, come with me. I need you to watch Nilbo and Schilling from the wings. Keep an eye on

anyone who seems surprised or upset that "Lotta" is on stage."
Violet flew out the door and up the stairs into the blackness of
backstage. She felt her way to the tree, already in place behind the
large upstage curtain, just as Lotta's pre-act music died away.

Until now, caught up in her 'mission,' she hadn't really
given much thought to what she was about to do. The stage grew
dark and she felt the breathless anticipation of the audience. Her
palms were wet as she held onto the tree, and her tongue was
paper-dry. Breathing rapidly, she could feel her heart race against
the thin material of her costume. Her costume! She was appearing
in public in next to nothing! What would everyone think! What
would her husband, Roger—her thought was cut short by the blare
of music and light that signaled Lotta's act. Suddenly calm, Violet
rolled the tree into place. It *was* Lotta's act, and everyone thought
she was Lotta. So she would *be* Lotta. With her natural grace and
impeccable memory, Violet mimicked the apple act flawlessly.
One exciting moment when she nearly dropped the large apple-
ball, then she completed the performance. She bowed at the
applause and blew kisses the way Lotta had, then ran into the
wings.

Leary stood with Nilbo and Schilling, both in handcuffs, by
the Stage Manager's podium.

"What you told me, and what I overheard while "Lotta"
was performing, was enough." Leary smiled. "The police are on
their way. You might want to put on some clothes."

Violet flushed and ran to change.

Lotta stirred on her settee. "Wass going on, honey? Why
are you dressed like that? Jeez my head hurts."

"Lotta, you passed out. I'll explain later, but just know
you're fine, your act's fine and I've got to change." Seeing Lotta's
baleful glare, she added, "No, I don't want your job, but this was
an emergency, believe me." Violet changed quickly, and ran up the
stairs. Stanley pointed to the alley and she dashed out the side

door, where a policeman was loading Nilbo and Schilling into a paddy wagon.

Leary said, "I found proof that Nilbo's plan was to force the performers out and turn the theatre into a movie house."

Violet finished the story. "Schilling found out and blackmailed him, so Nilbo got him to do his dirty work. Both nicely in each other's pockets. Can you believe it?" The policeman shook his head and drove away.

"Well, Miss Strange, your little show back there is one for the books."

"I expect complete confidentiality, Mr. Leary. The audience thought they were seeing Lotta Apples, and it's vital to the contracts of the Palace Performers that they continue to do so. Are we understood?"

"Sure, but it looked to me like you were having a good time. You weren't too bad, either."

"That, Mr. Leary, will also remain a secret."

◆ ◆ ◆

Author's Note

Violet Strange is a character originally written by Anna Katherine Green in the 1900s. Her work is in the public domain, however, I have written the story to fit her style and the timeline of her character's existence. In other words, this *could* be a lost work.

Victoria Heckman's first *Hawai'i mystery series* features officer Katrina Ogden, K.O., of the Honolulu Police Department. Her second series, *Coconut Man mysteries of Ancient Hawai'i* begins with *Kapu-Sacred*. Her newest work, *Burn Out,* is a stand alone mystery starring animal communicator Elizabeth Murphy. She is president of the Central Coast Chapter of Sisters in Crime. Visit her website http://www.victoriaheckman.com or email her at vheckman@charter.net

A Yellow Rose

Lori Hines

A used bookstore café with worn leather sofas, endless rows of books and a small coffee bar. A handsome man with shoulder length dark wavy hair peered at her repeatedly from behind a hardcover book. He wore short, baggy knee pants with a brown, round-necked schoolboy sweater. Camilla sensed immediately that there was something very special about him.

She flashed her sensual smile. A deliberate enticement. Within five minutes, he had mustered the courage to approach her.

"Excuse me," Barry said in a hesitant, yet somehow seductive, voice. "I just noticed your exquisite pentagram amulet." He stared at the necklace.

Could he be? Camilla wondered.

She held out the necklace so he could get a closer look. "A pewter pentacle bordered in Celtic knot work, set with a Swarovski crystal. It's an antique passed down from my grandmother."

"Stunning," he said. He gazed into her eyes.

She stared back at him with intensity and passion. "It represents…"

"Growth, prosperity and fertility," he finished.

He has to be pagan. I've been waiting over five years. After Richard left me on my birthday, I thought I'd never want another man again. Apparently 1932 is the year for love, as the stars predicted.

"That's not all," she responded excitedly, slipping her ankle out from under the table. She watched his gaze drift from her well-toned leg revealed beneath her long, slightly flared skirt, to her slender ankle with a Celtic spiral tattoo.

"Please sit down," Camilla said, using her long leg to push out the opposite chair. "So, are you pagan, or wiccan and pagan?"

"Both," he responded. "I grew up in a pagan home. We're all solitary though, no covens. My family felt we didn't need a group of other wiccans with whom to practice our rituals and Sabbats."

"Of course not." She leaned towards him. "The most powerful are those who are solitary."

They had talked nonstop for hours. Suddenly, he produced a glorious yellow rose. *Where did it come from*, she thought. I didn't see it at his table, or when he came over.

"This," he said, "is for new beginnings. After all, it is a Gibbous moon. Rather appropriate, don't you think?"

"Absolutely." She inhaled the sweet scent of the flower. "New ventures, new relationships."

* * * *

That was how it all began; in an unassuming Irish café two years earlier. They swore it would never end.

Camilla watched a herd of red deer graze next to the spectacular lake, while green rolling hills greeted the early morning mist. She had returned to the Victorian garden where her husband proposed.

After an hour of wandering the gardens, she approached the familiar limestone grotto path that meandered around a pond with a magnificent magnolia tree hanging overhead. A group of bright orange and crème koi welcomed her at the edge. They swam along beside her, peeking out from under the water lilies, vying for her attention.

As she waited anxiously, memories of that day wafted through her mind like the captivating, delicate pink blossoms floating on the water's surface. *Her hand softly rested in his, while he leaned down on one knee holding an emerald diamond ring set in a pentacle background—to match her necklace. "Wishes do come true," he said. "Because I found you. It's more than love – it's pure magic."*

They had eloped that very weekend.

Now the koi pursed their lips repeatedly as if desperately trying to tell her a secret. Then they scattered under the shallow water as her husband ran full force towards the garden, breathless and anxious.

Camilla smiled.

Barry ran through the entrance to the walled garden in eager anticipation, and approached the pagoda with a view of Knock Ion, the beautiful conical hill next to Lough Derravaragh which sits on the River Inny. He closed his eyes and deeply inhaled her sweet honeysuckle scent.

In a choked voice, "Camilla, Is it really you? I've been praying, hoping I could see you again." Barry looked directly at her. "You were always the one. After you disappeared…" He collapsed on his knees in front of her. "And right before our first anniversary."

Leaning over, she kissed him lightly on the lips. "Happy second anniversary, my love." She stroked the strong hand that reached out towards her face in disbelief, placing it against her right cheek. Then she handed him a single yellow rose.

* * * *

In disbelief, Barry picked up the flower Camilla had given him, holding it lovingly. His right hand trembled, and his slate blue eyes gazed at her. At that moment, the sun peeked out from behind the early morning clouds.

This feels heavy, he thought, glancing down inside the petals and curves. The rose contained the amulet that first caught his attention years ago—now a part of the flower. The emerald crystal was perfectly poised in the middle, glinting brilliantly from the sun's rays, making the stunning yellow of the rose pale in comparison.

A brief wind whispered through the magnolia tree, creating a cascade of pink petals that sprinkled down on both of them.

"Your beauty, your grace, your magic...I could hardly believe it when I so clearly dreamed of you here. Then when I found those yellow rose petals on our bed." A single tear rolled down his face.

"I came back to tell you that I didn't desert you," she whispered, placing her hands on his face. "You were the only one I ever loved."

"Everyone told me you ran off. But I knew it couldn't have been," Barry continued. "The police—they couldn't find your body."

"That's why I returned—to let you know that my death was a tragic accident. Nothing more. They couldn't find my body because they didn't know where to look. I discovered ancient ruins on that early morning hike near Ross Castle. Something told me not to go down that hidden trail, but you know I couldn't resist."

Smiling sadly, he only nodded his head.

"Honey, I was walking around on the foundation of a crumbling castle and fell through into an underground chamber."

Barry buried his face in his hands. He looked up and noticed tears flowed freely down both sides of her face.

"I should have told you where I was going. But it was a last minute walk while you were still sleeping in the hotel. I had no idea exploring ancient ruins would end in my demise."

His voice choked. "Where's your body Camilla? I can't rest until I put you to rest."

"I was buried alive. Some of the structure caved in on me when I fell.

My death was instantaneous. I can't tell you where it was. You'll know."

As she started to fade before his eyes, becoming one with the last of the morning mist, he heard, "You won't be alone, my love. Your rituals and requests have served more purpose than you know."

He realized it wasn't her last message. The tall square tower of Ross Castle and surrounding stone walls invaded his mind as clearly as if he were standing in front of it. The place they had stayed while on vacation.

Barry hailed a cab—a royal blue Low Loader taxi all the rage then. "Take me to Ross Castle," he said breathlessly. There was an unusual urgency to get there. He wanted to visit her final resting place.

"Thanks," he said, quickly giving the driver a 50 pound note. He found himself hurrying towards an unfamiliar trail along the shore of Lough Sheelin. Without thinking, he entered another smaller side trail that wasn't marked. Winding its way through trees, hills and valleys, the trail continued for a mile. At the end of the foot wide path, he saw the ruins.

She wanted me to find this place, he thought. *She wants me to put her to rest.*

The remnants of a small stone structure stood among the green hills with matching boulders and rocks scattered around the roofless building. A square foundation within fifty feet of the first stone ruin caught his attention. He stared into a dark pit with disintegrated sections of cement and stone.

He collapsed on his knees. "Oh Camilla, how do I get you out of there?"

Then he detected the sweet honeysuckle scent.

He hadn't seen the woman on the trail, and didn't remember her being there when he arrived. She had walked out of the single-room ruin. Barry gasped. The silky brown hair blowing in the breeze, long legs, and her olive skin...for a split second, he wondered if his spells to bring Camilla back to life had worked.

"Hello," she said.

As soon as she spoke, he realized she couldn't be his deceased wife. This woman's voice had a lighter tone. Camilla's was sultry.

"Did you need some help?" the mysterious beauty asked. "You seem as confused as I am about being here."

"Yes," he whispered in astonishment. "Where did you come from?"

She played with her necklace nervously. "I'm staying at Ross Castle, on vacation with some girlfriends from the states. It was so weird. I was out roaming the grounds, then I had this sudden urge to go walking behind the property, practically running here all the way. This has to be over two miles from there, and it's not easy to find."

Barry saw her looking at the yellow rose lying next to him. He stood up to shake her hand. "Hello, my name's Barry, Barry Pierson." Her eyes were the same emerald as the pendant still buried in the rose. He could barely breathe as he gazed into them.

"I'm Jade," she said. They continued to hold hands for a few seconds. Then Barry thought he heard something move by his feet.

"What happened to your flower?" she asked. "It was right there a few seconds ago."

A spot of yellow in the depths of the collapsed foundation caught his eye. Kneeling down again, he saw the rose Camilla had given him lying atop the rubble where she lay buried.

A whisper on the wind spoke to him, though Jade didn't seem to notice.

"New ventures, new relationships," the sultry voice said. "After all, it's a Gibbous moon."

♦ ♦ ♦

Lori Hines is a member of Sisters in Crime, Desert Sleuths Chapter, the Arizona Archaeological Society, Aqua Fria Chapter, and the Arizona Authors Association. Her mysteries are inspired by experiences as a paranormal investigator. Lori is working on her second novel in *The Ancient Ones* series, titled *Caves of the Watchers*. Readers can visit her online at http://www.lhauthor.wordpress.com.

Uncertain Sanctuary

Sue McGinty

Piedras Blancas Lightstation, California Central Coast, 1939

The day I discovered the body began quietly, with breakfast for the three bachelor lightkeepers and chores for me, a girl of sixteen years, their only servant. Mid-morning brought a short walk to the garden to gather vegetables for supper. As always I was accompanied by a yellow mongrel known only as Dog. No one knew from where he came or how long he had been at the light station. Perhaps, like me, he had a secret.

I hurried the short distance from the cottage to the almost-barren garden keeping an eye on the leaden November sky. *Rain coming soon.* I forced myself to think in English, the better to guard against a careless slip of the tongue.

As we walked Dog moved closer, wagging his tail in an arc that brushed my leg. He often seemed to understand my thoughts, and his brief touch eased my lonely heart. We were a pair, were Dog and I.

Nearing the garden, I found myself, as always, mesmerized by the lighthouse, a conical tower of one hundred and seventy-four feet, stark white and trimmed in black. Its beam flashed twice every fifteen seconds, a beacon for ships plying the waters off the rocky coast. Night after night those flashes invaded my dreams, which were already troubled by fears of men living without women.

Though I could not see above the eight foot wall erected to break the wind, I knew that beyond it stretched a seascape that might have been transported from the oceans of the moon. White rocks with curious flat tops—fit only for migratory birds and seals—sat offshore. The barren point jutted into the ocean, as though to escape the land.

As I had done when I fled my birth country.

With Dog waiting patiently, I gathered a few scrawny carrots and tough onions from the tiny patch planted by a previous keeper's wife. Other ingredients for our meals came from supplies delivered every three months by ship to the wharf at the south end of the point.

The rain intensified. "We'd better get back, Dog."

Clutching my meager harvest beneath my slicker, I started for the cottage where I slept in a small attic room. Lars, the head keeper, occupied the downstairs. The assistant keepers lived in larger quarters, but took their meals in Lars' dining room. I ate alone in the kitchen.

Dog remained at my side, apparently willing to endure bad weather for good company, or any company at all. The keepers ignored him except to boot him in the ass when it suited them.

Close now to the cottage, I looked down on the wharf so vital to our existence. Beyond and to the left across a small bay lay a small inlet with a sandy beach.

"Let's go there someday, my friend. We can take a picnic lunch." Dog nudged the side of my knee with his nose.

Such an outing would involve risk, for Lars had forbidden me to leave the compound. But he was often gone, the others tending the light or sleeping in preparation for night duty in the watch room. One keeper must be on duty at all times, no exceptions.

The assistants ignored me except to growl their displeasure: Cedric's toast burned, Michel's coffee cold. Swiss they were, including Lars.

Except for Red, the only American. As third assistant he tended the fog signal building. Red of hair and face, big of chest, kind of eye, he brought me newspapers and magazines, including *National Geographic* and the popular new *Life*, from the supply ship. The ship also brought novels, though he was the only keeper who read them.

Red was a mystery fan. With a wink and a comment like, "You'll love the new Miss Marple," he passed them to me on the sly. Lars viewed reading for pleasure as a vice.

But Red had been gone for several days and no one had explained his absence. Without him the light station was short one keeper.

I stopped, attracted to something on the beach of the inlet. Its shape stirred a familiar unease within me. Dog paused as well. I dumped the vegetables into an untidy heap on the stoop and we ran to the southern point.

I gazed across the bay, studying the object. Except that it wasn't an object, but a human body.

I'd seen dead people, too many, on *Kristallnacht*, a Nazi pogrom against Jews throughout Germany and Austria, the year before. The man lay sideways on the beach, arms akimbo, head at an unnatural angle. A fisherman thrown from his boat? Not unheard of in these dangerous waters. Or could it be Red? Impossible to tell from where I stood.

Dog whimpered beside me. My eyes focused on the highway. A truck. Lars. He would know what to do.

I waited at the end of the auto trestle that connected the highway to the light station property. The trestle was built above the dunes to keep motor cars from sinking into the sand. My stomach churned and my knees knocked together. As soon as he heard the truck engine, Dog ran off, tail between his legs. As the truck approached, I ran alongside.

Lars' ice blue eyes widened as though I'd taken leave of my senses. "What the—?"

"Sir, sir, something has happened."

Lines furrowed his pale forehead. "The light?" His blonde moustache twitched as his eyes shot toward the lighthouse.

"No, no." I pointed a thumb over my shoulder at the inlet, hardly able to force the words out. "A…A body…On the beach."

Should I tell him it might be Red? No, that would not be smart.

"A body? Impossible," he said, groping for the field glasses he always carried. He hurried slightly ahead of me to the point above the wharf and raised the glasses to his eyes. This act released an animal smell from beneath his arms that further roiled my stomach. It was often so when he stood close to me.

He turned. "Silly girl," he said, shaking his head, his clipped hair riffling like shorn wheat in the worsening wind. "It's only a seal."

I looked again. "It hasn't moved."

"A *dead* seal, not a body. You fill your head with nonsense from Agatha Christie novels." He turned on his heel and strode toward the lighthouse. I always hid my books in my dresser drawer when I left my room. Lars had been there, his hands pawing through my things.

I shivered, and not from the cold.

* * * *

After dinner at noon, I prepared for supper by setting the soup pot in the deep well cooker of the wood stove. I then retreated to my room hoping to begin a new mystery. My thoughts allowed for no such luxury that day.

I drew back the freshly laundered lace curtain, which smelled of the outdoors, where it had been dried, and peered out my east-facing dormer window (the other faced the lighthouse) at the highway and the barren hills beyond. Leaning my forehead on the glass, I reflected for the thousandth time on how I'd arrived at this uncertain sanctuary.

Three months ago, bruised and bleeding from the bus accident that killed my parents, I'd walked miles to a Salinas orphanage and presented myself, not as the Jewish refuge I was, but as Astrid Cole. Astrid for my Swedish grandmother, Cole because an Anglo-Saxon surname, especially when accompanied by blonde braids, was more valuable than gold, even in a country far from Nazi Germany.

But my constant book-reading and endless questions—the legacy of professor parents—were too much for women of a Christian God accustomed to well-behaved Mexican children. The good sisters, meaning well, but innocent in the ways of the world, had dispatched me to this place with no questions asked or answered. I had no papers; in a panic, I'd left them behind with my dead parents.

My room lay directly above Lars'. At night I heard his restless stirrings; it was only a matter of time until he forced himself on me. He was a man with no woman, and I, at sixteen, a juicy peach ripe for plucking.

* * * *

Without warning Lars' truck pulled up and stopped a short distance below my window. Cedric drove, with Lars in the passenger seat. He hopped out and began gesturing toward the road and the cove as though giving Cedric directions.

My heart skipped a beat, then another as I gaze down upon a truck bed loaded with several cement blocks, coiled rope and a large tarpaulin. Cedric drove off and Lars headed toward the wharf area on foot.

What was going on?

Several minutes later I spied Lars rowing one of the skiffs across the bay toward the cove.

Was this what I thought it was? Were they going to weigh and wrap the body, then dump it far out to sea?

The only way to find out was to watch them from the point above the wharf. I dashed down the stairs, but just as a I reached the front door, I heard a voice from behind.

"Girl, I was just coming to fetch you. Fix me a cup of coffee."

I jumped and whirled around. Michel stood in the kitchen doorway. He'd left the light untended. Was keeping an eye on me more important than remaining on duty?

I stared into his face and got no answers.

* * * *

Cedric showed up on time for supper, but Lars arrived late, cold and wet, as one would expect if he'd been out on the ocean. Michel was on duty and the other two ate silently, eyes on their plates. Did they have any idea of what I'd seen from my window?

* * * *

For the next few days, terrified, worried and feeling vulnerable indeed, I went about my tasks. Red remained absent, vanished as had the body in the cove. At night he scattered his laughter like stardust into my fearful dreams, making them bearable. Except when he whispered, "Listen, girl, listen."

What was I to listen to? The late-night voices from the downstairs parlor? Because of the constant sound of the fog signal in the foul November weather, I could not hear what they said, only their deep guttural tones. These conversations were conducted while smoking endless cigarettes, the smell of which drifted into my dreams. The men also consumed large quantities of whiskey that caused them to cradle their heads the next morning.

* * * *

The new third assistant arrived at week's end, Johannes by name, blonde, blue-eyed, Swiss like the rest. The man had an older, wiser look to him, even more so than Lars, who was an old man of forty. Why would such a man as Johannes take such a position?

Not for me to wonder. America still suffered the effects of an economic Depression that had lasted for nine years. Many people gladly accepted jobs below their status.

Like the others, he spoke with a slight accent. Did any of them notice that I too spoke with a similar accent? So unlike our occasional visitors who spoke in voices of the American west, and who, like Red, had ready smiles and kind eyes.

My parents were professors of Germanic languages and, early on, I'd developed an ear for speech patterns. Because of this, I knew the keepers were from the part of Switzerland where *Schweizerdeutsch* was spoken. But I'd never heard the steely-eyed keepers utter a word of that dialect, even inadvertently. What if I, in a lapsed moment, said something in German, the language of my birth?

Or worse, Hebrew, the language of my heart?

* * * *

Cedric and Michel slept in the two tiny downstairs bedrooms of their cramped quarters, while Johannes occupied the upstairs room that had been Red's. He had always thanked me for cleaning his room, but his successor kept his door closed and locked tight. (I had checked.) Fine with me, I had more than enough to do.

Early one evening, a week after Johannes arrived, I was on my knees in the keepers' parlor, scrubbing away muddy footprints— and thinking that no wonder these men had no wives—when the emergency telephone rang. The instrument connected the watch room to all the main buildings and its ring could only mean trouble. I jumped at the shrill sound, almost upsetting the pail of water beside me.

Cedric, the first assistant, answered. "Yes, Lars?" His brows knitted together. "Johannes, Michel and I will be there directly."

Some emergency involving the light. With no beacon to guide them, ships offshore would be in grave danger after dark. All keepers needed immediately. Michel left immediately while Cedric yelled for Johannes who flew down the stairs. Together the men ran out the door.

As I closed the door against the driving wind and rain, I spied Dog huddled on the stoop. Forbidden access to the house, he glanced at me with mournful eyes. "Come inside," I said, "and warm yourself." He didn't resist, shaking himself on my freshly scrubbed floor as I slammed the door behind him.

"Look at what you've done!" I said, grabbing a rag and wiping first him, and then the floor. But I was grateful for his company and returned to my chores, confident the men would be gone long enough for Dog to warm his bones.

Sometime later, kitchen chores complete, I moved back into the parlor, drying my hands on a towel. The room was empty. "Dog?"

A floorboard creaked overhead, and my heart skipped a beat. Johannes? No, he would have made his presence known. It could only be Dog.

I ascended the stairs two at a time and, sure enough, found Johannes had left his bedroom door ajar. I hesitated, hardly daring to look inside, yet unable to stop myself. I pushed the door open with the flat of my hand and crossed the threshold.

Johannes' room was neat, excessively so, his clothes hung on the wire rack, (unlike Red's which were either scattered on the floor or tossed into his suitcase), pillows plumped, blankets tucked in with military precision.

A shuffling noise came from under the bed. "Is that you, Dog?" More shuffling and a whine. I got down on hands and knees and peered under the bed. He had taken refuge behind a large suitcase, one ear, one eye and a tail visible.

"Come out of there." He didn't budge. I dragged the suitcase out in order to get at him.

What was this? Dog forgotten, I stared at the black leather valise. It was unlatched. *Dare I?* Quickly I threw it open before I lost my nerve.

Inside was a radio. *A radio.* Why would Johannes have such a thing? And in a suitcase under his bed? It was smaller than the one in our Berlin apartment, but with more dials. Connected to it was a device I'd seen in *Life* magazine, a microphone used for broadcasting. What other secrets did that man keep under his bed?

I again lifted the blanket. Dog had moved behind another suitcase, pushed way back. Sweating and shaking, I dragged it out. I stared at it, alarm pounding in my temples.

I'd seen it often enough, it belonged to Red. He would never go away and leave his suitcase behind. I understood then that Red's had been the body on the beach, dispatched to a watery grave by Lars in the lightstation skiff after Cedric returned to the house for dinner on the night in question.

Sick with fear, I shoved both suitcases back under the bed and dragged Dog into the hall and shooed him downstairs, stopping only to shut Johannes' door with my foot.

I pushed the protesting animal out into the cold and rain, trying to make sense of the radio. Perhaps it provided an alternate means of communication in this remote location. That would make sense. Why then did they not use it to warn others of problems with the light? And why keep Red's suitcase under the bed? Perhaps the keepers had forgotten its presence.

* * * *

"Mr. Hearst will bring two female visitors, one of whom, Miss Marion Davies, has been here before, to the light station next Tuesday," Lars announced the next morning. "They will join us for dinner at noon and then tour the lighthouse." The assistants exchanged a look registering their displeasure at the intrusion.

I stopped ladling out the breakfast oatmeal long enough to wonder what the visit would mean for me. More work surely, and I would not be asked to join them at table. But female company would be nice, if only to observe their dresses and coiffures and smell their cologne.

Astrid, how you could you think such a thing when your life is in danger?

But that thought lead to another more productive one: Perhaps company would provide a means of escape.

I'd read about Mr. Hearst and his enormous ranch five miles south on the highway. He published newspapers said to influence powerful men, especially those opposed to President Roosevelt. Of course, I had no idea what that would mean for me, but the man must hold sway with the authorities.

Lars' thin lips tightened. "Girl, you have one week to make this place shine like a soldier's boots."

* * * *

Later, I was standing by the sink, washing up, when I felt a presence and turned. Johannes. "Did you shut the door yesterday afternoon?"

My heart skipped a beat. "Of course, sir. In your haste, you left it open and the rain was coming in."

An impatient sigh. "Not the front door, my bedroom door."

Caught. I thought fast. "Of course not, sir. I was downstairs the whole time you were gone."

Doubt flickered in his eyes.

* * * *

In the next week I polished metal, scrubbed wood, and dusted cobwebs until my back ached and my fingers turned raw from the lye soap. I dropped into bed at night too exhausted to even dream, much less formulate a plan of escape.

On the night before the guests arrived, I lay deep in sleep, not caring if the beam from the lighthouse flashed into my west-facing window every fifteen seconds, or that the fog signal had grown silent for once.

Suddenly I awoke. A footfall on the stairs. I sat up.

Please don't let it be Lars coming to have his way with me.

A creak as the intruder hit a loose board on the stairs.

Pretend to sleep, Astrid.

I lay back down and turned away so that Lars would not see me blink when the beam hit my face. My heart beat furiously as he twisted the knob (for there was no lock) and the door opened.

I felt his eyes upon me and I smelled his familiar animal scent. My skin crawled as though alive with ants.

I waited, holding my breath.

Then he closed the door. His footsteps retreated, the creaking stair protesting under his weight.

About to explode, I exhaled.

Why did he come in here? Had he been in my room before, watching me sleep?

* * * *

Sometime later, the fog horn and familiar male voices, an urgent tone to their words, roused me from a fitful sleep.

Another emergency?

I tiptoed to the door and opened it a crack, straining to hear.

The words were garbled, but I realized with a jolt that they were speaking high German, not the *Schweizerdeutsch* of the Germanic Swiss.

My heart dropped to my toes. I had read that German-speakers in America were often Nazi spies. Surely there was some logical explanation other than that. What could it be? And why pass themselves off as Swiss? If indeed they were indeed Nazis, I must find out why they were here.

I slipped out the door and stood in the dark at the top of the stairs. The voices were louder, though not enough to hear the exact words. I took a step down, and then another, still in darkness. I hoped one of them would not pass the stairwell on the way to the toilet, or the kitchen for more whiskey.

I heard the phrase, *befehl des Fuehrer's*, "order of the Fuehrer."

My breath caught in my chest. I gulped air and chanced another step down.

The stair creaked.

Conversation stopped.

I stiffened, listening.

"Only the wind," one said in German and they resumed their discussion.

I heard Lars address Johannes as "Your Excellency."

Why that term of respect for a lowly third assistant? Perhaps, no certainly, Johannes was not who he pretended to be. A high official? I thought about the radio in the suitcase. Could there be a connection between it and this urgent meeting?

How could there not be?

Lars and Johannes continued to argue, their voices rising. I heard *Kaiser in Japan,* "Emperor of Japan."

What did the Emperor Hirohito have to do with four lightkeepers on the remote central coast of California? My mind could not wrap itself around such an idea.

I remained in the shadows long enough to learn that Johannes was to make contact with, and then board, a Japanese submarine, *Das U-Boot*, off Piedras Blancas the following evening. The argument concerned whether, if there was a storm, Lars would ferry him to the rendezvous in his skiff. Johannes insisted it had to be then, no matter the risk. The submarine would not, could not, wait.

I'd heard enough. Numb with fear and cold, I could only escape to my room. As I turned to do so, my foot tangled in the hem of my nightgown. Down I went.

"What the hell?" Lars, followed by the others, ran from the parlor.

I stood up, rubbing my backside. "The toilet, sir. I needed to use the toilet. I fell on the stairs."

* * * *

Unable to form a rational plan, I spent a sleepless night terrified that Lars would kill me in my bed. The next morning as I went about emptying ashtrays and clearing glasses, the keepers, Lars especially, stared at me with suspicious eyes. Had Johannes conveyed to him his doubts about closing his bedroom door? Unlikely, for that would show carelessness on his part.

Still, my life was in danger as Red's must have surely been. Had he discovered their secret? Or was he merely an inconvenience, killed to make way for Johannes? One thing was certain: They might not know I spoke German, but they must understand that anyone short of an idiot could discern a conversation sprinkled with *Heil Hitlers*.

No matter the risk, I needed to speak to Mr. Hearst today. What if he refused to take me seriously? Or worse, told Lars?

Perhaps I should use the emergency telephone instead. As far as I knew, it connected only the watch room to the main buildings, but perhaps one could reach the outside operator on it. Lars had already announced that during the tour Michel would stay behind, most certainly to watch me. There would be no opportunity to try the telephone.

As I placed the dinner ham into the deep-well cooker, set bread to rise, peeled potatoes for mashing, and made sauce from butter, cinnamon and dried apples, I formed a plan driven by fury.

* * * *

"Still as quaint as ever," remarked Miss Marion Davies from the front entrance. I paused from setting the dining room table, fork in hand, seeing through her eyes a low-ceilinged, smallish room with clean lace curtains, rose-patterned wallpaper, overstuffed, furniture, and colorful rugs crocheted by the wives of former keepers.

"Isn't it?" announced her companion, introduced as film star Carole Lombard. Both ladies were blonde and blue-eyed, what a good German would call "*Zaftig*." Cedric and Michel stared at the two women hungrily. Johannes was on duty.

"And Mister Hearst?" asked Lars, smitten like the rest of them.

"Oh," said Miss Davies with a dismissive wave, "he's in New York on business." She took Lars' arm and tucked it under her own. I thought he would have a stroke. "It's just us today."

My heart sank. I had hoped that he was merely late. These flighty women would be of no help.

Lars patted her hand. "And your chauffeur, Madame? Would he like to wait in the garage? A storm is expected." He peered out the window with a worried expression.

No wonder. A storm coming and a rendezvous tonight.

Miss Davies raised a well-penciled eyebrow. "You would relegate my chauffeur to the garage, sir?"

"No, no Madame. I only meant—"

"It doesn't matter what you meant. I drove my roadster today."

Aha! She drove her own motor car.

Lars' eyes widened. "And how did you deal with the gates Madame?"

Mr. Hearst had placed a series of barbed wire gates which had to be opened and closed separately across the highway from the Hearst property to Piedras Blancas.

Miss Davies and Miss Lombard exchanged glances. "Carole took care of them."

Lars turned to Miss Lombard. "And you closed them properly, Madame? Mr. Hearst would be very angry if those gates were left open."

Another exchanged glance. Miss Lombard said, "Of course."

Lars nodded, apparently satisfied. He again peered out the window and turned to me, still in the dining room, still with the same fork in hand. "The storm will arrive later this afternoon. You will delay the meal for two hours while we tour the lighthouse and grounds."

"Yes, sir." Two hours to change my plan. I eyed the blonde, glamorous film stars. Perhaps they were stronger than they looked.

* * * *

The tour took longer than expected. It was close to three when the women and all the keepers except Johannes, who was still on duty, gathered round the table. My hands shook as I served ham from the platter. In my apron pocket was a note telling of events here and asking for help. I chose Miss Davies as the recipient because she lived at the ranch.

Standing over her left shoulder, and keeping one eye on Lars, I balanced the tray of sliced meat in one hand. With the other, I dug into my pocket. Just as my fingers grasped the folded paper, alas, I overreached. The platter tipped, grazing the woman's shoulder and spilling ham into her lap.

I stood there with the empty platter, frozen with horror, aghast at what I'd done.

All was lost.

"Oh, oh, oh," Miss Davies cried, standing and groping for a napkin to wipe her frock.

Speechless, I watched Lars rise from the chair and advance toward me. "*Dúmmes Maedel!*" Teeth-jarring, searing pain shot through my skull as he backhanded me across the face, first on one cheek and then the other. "Get to the kitchen."

Miss Lombard said, "You dimwit." I assumed her words were for me and fled the room, tears scalding my eyes.

I stood at the sink, trying to catch my breath between sobs. My clumsiness had made passing the note impossible. These women would leave and I would disappear, as had Red.

I leaned over, clutched my midsection and cried from fear. I cried from the humiliation of being considered a dumb girl. I cried for Red. I cried for my dead parents, the first tears I'd shed since they died.

I cried until a floral scent tickled my nose and I felt a hand on my shoulder. The warmth of it penetrated my skin.

"You poor kid." I turned and stepped into the waiting arms of Miss Davies. My mind dimly registered Miss Lombard standing in the doorway.

"I...I have to escape," I whispered into Miss Davies' ear.

She stepped back, grabbed my forearms and gently shook them. "Of course you do. These men are brutes."

"More than that. They're--"

Lars now stood in the doorway behind Miss Lombard. He pushed her aside. She said a most unladylike word.

"Unfortunately, ladies, the tour has ended. I will escort you to your automobile." He glared at me, hatred and—could it be?—fear in his eyes. "Get to your room. I'll deal with you later."

"Yes sir, the tour *has* ended, sir," said Miss Lombard, "and this young lady is coming with us." She moved toward me until I stood flanked by both women who seemed to grow taller as they stood with me.

"No, no, that's impossible," Lars shouted. "She's an indentured servant. I am responsible for her welfare. You have no right…"

"Bullshit," said Miss Davies. "she's coming with us. No matter what the reason, I will not allow her to remain here." She paused. "Mr. Hearst and his newspaper empire will guarantee her safety. I'm sure you don't want his reporters swarming around this place."

Miss Davies, you are so right about that.

Lars opened and closed his mouth several times, like a fish gasping for air. Then he found his voice. And made a mistake. "Cedric, Michel, fetch Johannes! Quickly." The keepers nodded and quickly departed.

With Lars alone, the balance of power had shifted. "Let's get out of here while we can," muttered Miss Lombard. The ladies each grabbed an arm and marched me toward the door. I glanced over my shoulder at Lars, imagining his thoughts: he and Johannes had an important rendezvous in a few hours. On the one hand, I would tell what I knew, on the other, if the two women failed to return, powerful forces would be unleashed.

"Go," he said, as if it were of little consequence. His eyes conveyed quite a different message: what would happen when the keepers returned.

* * * *

Darkness came early that stormy day, but had not quite descended when we dashed to the automobile in driving rain. Miss Lombard, hair plastered to her head, climbed into the passenger seat next to Miss Davies who sat behind the wheel drumming her fingers. "Come on, come on."

I scrambled in closest to the passenger door, a pretty tight squeeze, even though Miss Lombard and I were both slim. Terrified at what we'd done, I craned my neck and peered out the back window. Backlit by the parlor lamp, Lars lurched through the open doorway. "Hurry! He's not waiting for the rest. He's coming after us."

Miss Davies pulled the choke. The engine caught, sputtered. And died.

"Hurry!"

She jammed the pedal to the floor. "I'm trying, kid."

I looked again. Lars approaching fast. "He's going to get us. He might have a gun."

"Shut up, kid. You're making me nervous."

Finally, the engine turned over and caught. We spewed Lars with mud as Miss Davies made a half-turn and we headed for the trestle. He shook his fist, reminding me of Adolph Hitler.

I leaned out the window and glimpsed Lars now heading the opposite way, toward his truck. We had to get over the trestle. If he rammed us from behind, our lighter automobile would topple into the dunes. "Please hurry."

Miss Davies let out a sigh that fogged the front window.

I looked again. Lars nowhere in sight. In the truck? Gone to fetch the other keepers?

No. On the ground.

Something tore at his leg. I looked again, forcing my eyes to focus through the rain. Dog. He'd taken Lars down. "Stop," I yelled to Miss Davies.

"What the hell?" she exclaimed, but she lurched to a stop just short of the trestle. I forced the door open against the wind and hopped outside. Lars was still on the ground. "Dog," I yelled, waving, "Come *on*."

He didn't seem to understand. "Come *here*!" Ears back, he bounded straight to the car and jumped into the front seat, spraying Miss Davies and Miss Lombard with water and mud. I hopped in and clasped my arms around him. My last glimpse of Lars in the rearview mirror showed him hobbling behind us.

Miss Davies came to the end of the trestle and turned south onto the highway. "Oh no!" I said, "the gates."

"What about them?"

"I know Lars. He'll get his truck and catch us if we have to open and close each gate. He's done it many times."

"Nonsense," said Miss Davies, maneuvering through the gears, "we left them open. We weren't going to ruin our dresses on that barbed wire. Besides," she took her hand off the gearshift and patted the steering wheel, "this little baby really moves when she has to."

* * * *

As we bumped and jolted our way along the newly completed Cabrillo Highway into the gathering darkness that stormy night so many years ago, I told my story to Miss Davies who promptly notified authorities. Of course, they hushed everything up. Later, the omnipotent Mr. Hearst told Miss Davies—who told me—that when the authorities got to Piedras Blancas, the station was deserted, the light untended, the radio gone. Red's body was never found.

Perhaps it was a coincidence, perhaps not, but shortly after the incident the United States Coast Guard assumed control of the lighthouse.

Despite the cover-up, rumors persist of a Japanese submarine sighting off Piedras Blancas that night. In 1940, Japan and Germany signed an Axis Pact. I still wonder whether there was some connection between that and the events I bore witness to in 1939. Did those evil men survive and make their way to Japan? We'll never know.

As for me, I became Miss Davies' social secretary at the ranch with no questions asked by Mr. Hearst. Dog joined the other animals at the compound during the day. When darkness fell, I brought him inside to sleep by the fire as I read my latest mystery, secure at last in the sanctuary provided by the ranch.

In 1994, with little more than a yen for beach living, a story idea, and a cat who'd never ridden in a car before, Sue McGinty left LA behind and headed north to the Central Coast town of Los Osos. Her short fiction has been featured in three Central Coast Mystery Writer anthologies and she has served as president and treasurer of Sisters in Crime, Central Coast Chapter. She also chairs the Lillian Dean Writing Competition at the Central Coast Writer's Conference. Her *Bella Kowalski* series includes *Murder in Los Lobos* (2008) and *Murder at Cuyamaca Beach* (2010).

Contact Sue at: http://www.SueMcGinty.com or Friend her on Facebook.

Perseverance

Nan Mahon

It was early Sunday morning, the air still cool and damp from overnight rain. The dawn's freshness was filled with scents of magnolia and roses in bloom. But a rising summer sun, streaking the blue sky with gold, promised to burn down on our little town in southern Georgia, so those who had work to do rose early. Still, the streets were quiet, William O'Rourke told us later down at the general store. Said he was perched on his milk wagon ambling through town when he came upon something that looked like a bundle of dirty clothes in the road. Cans and bottles rattled against each other as he pulled the reins and brought the two old bay horses to a stop. The hound dogs riding with him sat up on their haunches and sniffed the air. O'Rourke climbed off the wagon and the dogs jumped off behind him.

O'Rourke bent over a man's body and exclaimed, "Lord God almighty!"

He left his horses and wagon standing in the middle of the road and ran for the sheriff's office, his two big dogs right on his heels, barking so's to wake the devil himself. Sheriff Bradley and his deputy Art Monroe were drinking coffee, their boots up on the desk, when O'Rourke busted in yellin' about the body in the road. They strapped on gun belts, pulled on their hats, and took off after him back to where the milk wagon stood, the horses switchin' their tails at the flies comin' up from the body and gathering on them.

They stared dumbfounded at the man lying on the muddy ground in the middle of Second Street, a section of town where rich folks lived before the war and the Yankee reconstruction. The victim had caught a double-barrel blast in the face. But what shocked them most was that the gunman had taken an additional shot that blew the man's privates completely off.

"Cain't rightly tell who it is," said the sheriff.

"Lookie at that gold watch on his vest," Deputy Monroe said. "Good God! It's that Yankee officer."

The men stared at each other. The war had ended three years ago, but the Union army and especially that officer, whom we knew all too well, would always be the enemy to folks who lived in our town. Bitterness dwelt deep inside people whose way of life had been trampled and burned to the ground.

Just as astonishing, Amy Connors was in church that morning. The congregation tried not to stare when she came in and took her place in the family pew. For more than three years her seat had been empty and the townspeople had gotten used to her being a recluse in that once fine old house on Second Street.

Amy wore a spring dress of white polished cotton sprinkled with tiny blue flowers. Her straw hat was banded with the same material, her gloves a loose crochet, and a cameo on a silver chain rested against her throat. She looked like the month of May. She was thinner and paler than I remembered her, but her eyes were clear and bright as though a storm had passed through and the sun was out again.

I remembered when her sister Rosemary came into my general store and bought a bolt of that dress material. "I'm going to make a new dress for Amy. Maybe she will come out again if she has something pretty to show off."

I don't believe the dress brought Amy out of her self-imposed exile. It may have had something to do with the former Yankee Cavalry officer found dead in the street earlier that morning.

Oh yes, we all recognized him when he came back to town dressed in a three piece suit with a gold chain looped across his vest. He was not too different from the man in a dusty blue uniform and high black riding boots who came through Georgia with General George Sherman and his army.

As a store owner in a small Southern town I take pride in my ability to remember names and faces. I can tell you every man, woman and child in our community, including the names of their dogs. So when he came in about three weeks ago, I knew who he was right away.

"Surprised you'd come back down here," I said.

"Working for the railroad now," he answered. "War's over, we need to put all that behind us."

"Not likely," I muttered.

"Connors family still in that place on Second Street? Looks like it's gone to hell."

"Amy's there. Ya'll killed her daddy."

He made no reply, just took a sack of tobacco from the bin, plunked down some money on the counter and left.

He had first come riding into our town that summer of '64 with a company of hard-looking Union soldiers, the sun glinting on their sabers and rifles. The line of riders was so long it took them half an hour to pass through Main Street. The captain rode up front on a spirited gelding that tossed his head with every step. He stopped in front of that fine old house on Second Street and motioned all but a small squad to move on. He and his men dismounted, walked up on the porch and shot Henry Connor down on their way through the door. They made their headquarters in the Connor's house, keeping the two black servants and Amy as their prisoners.

Amy was just eighteen at the time, as pretty as the purple morning glories that climbed the trellis on the wrap-around porch of their house.

Three years before the Yankees came, Amy had promised to marry the Miller boy whose family lived just down the street. They had known each other all their lives and the day he marched off to war looking young and proud in his new gray uniform, she gave him a yellow ribbon from her hair and promised to wait for his return.

Most of the town turned out that morning to watch the men and boys line up in formation behind Major Luther McMahon on his dancing black mare. I remember the spring sun shining on Amy's long auburn hair. She was crying when she untied the ribbon and put it in Rob Miller's hand. He kissed the satin band and waved to her as the column moved down the road, raising a dust cloud that caught flight on a sudden breeze. We all were so sure they would be home victorious by plantin' time.

We were wrong.

News reached us some months later that Miller had been killed in a battle at a place we had never heard of. They buried him off somewhere too far for his family to ever visit or put a marker on his grave.

Then the war came to our town, to our front doors, and into the Connor house. Folks said the Captain made Amy his personal prize during the time he was there. Spoils of war some might say. We all tried not to think of the terrible things that were certainly happening to Amy inside her own house. We were helpless to come to her aid.

The soldiers camped in our pastures and bathed in our streams. Their horses grazed where they chose and dropped dung in the streets. Bonfires blazed high and sometimes at night laughter echoed across peach orchards and cotton fields. Just as often, the lonely sound of a harmonica filled the air. It crossed our minds that those young men, so far from home, might be homesick for their families just as our fighting boys must be. Just the same, we kept our daughters and young sons inside and out of sight.

The soldiers slaughtered the town's livestock, pigs and chickens and raided the grain silos. What they didn't eat they carried away in their chuck wagons for the long march through our state, looting and burning their way to the sea. When they finally left, we felt sick with relief as the long line of dirty blue disappeared down the road toward Savannah.

The town recovered slowly but Amy never left the house again. Not until this morning. That beautiful old two-story antebellum house went into neglect as the paint began to peel and weeds took over the front flower beds, garden and lawns. Matted straw seating rotted in empty porch rocking chairs. Even the morning glories retreated in despair. Offers from townspeople to help with repairs went unacknowledged.

Rosemary and Margret, Amy's married sisters, lived on farms outside town, as they had during the occupation. When it ended and the Union army cleared out, her sisters begged Amy to come live with one of them, but she refused, choosing to stay all alone in that big house. They came in my store occasionally to buy supplies for Amy, but they could not persuade her to come out of her self-imposed prison. Oh, sometimes a passerby might catch a glimpse of her working in the small vegetable garden behind her house. Church ladies who came calling with baskets of food, casseroles or baked goods had to leave them at the doorstep because their knocks were never answered. No one except her sisters came face to face with Amy until this morning; a day so clear and bright after a summer rain. Just a few hours earlier O'Rourke and the lawmen had found the captain laying on the muddy, red ground in the middle of Second Street.

The sheriff didn't spend any time looking for the killer.

"It could have been anyone," he said. "Everyone in these parts owns a shotgun and had reason to hate all the captain represented."

There was Bill Jackson who lost a leg at Shiloh, Aaron Miller who spent two long years starving in the Yankee prison camp in Andersonville, Jake Harper who had three sons killed in battle and Jack Snider who watched as his farm was burned to the ground by Sherman's men. We all spent a hard year scraping by after the captain and his men rode out with all our food. Yes sir, any of us could have done it. Quietly, we were glad.

"Oughta give 'em a medal," the people said.

"He had it comin' if anybody ever did," others agreed.

No one mentioned Amy or questioned why she came out of the house after all this time. Not even this morning when she walked silently down the aisle and took her place. The congregation was singing *Rock of Ages* when she came in and the voices faded as she walked past, surprise on people's faces. Brother Cable, our minister, stepped up to the podium and smiled directly at Amy.

"Blessed are those who persevere under trial," he quoted from the Book of James, chapter one.

The light shone through the stained-glass window and lit Amy's face as she sat holding a white Bible in her gloved hands. Maybe it was the sun that gave brightness to her eyes and the smile that played on her lips as the minister spoke of redemption and restitution for those who persevere.

♦ ♦ ♦

Nan Mahon is a journalist, author, writing instructor and community activist. She belongs to Capitol Crimes, the Sacramento Chapter of Sisters in Crime, and is on the Elk Grove Committee for the Arts. She likes to write a little on the dark side and has a passion for blues music.

Hidden Past

Gay Toltl Kinman

Los Olivos, California, 1882

The road was muddy as usual in the late spring with a hint of more rain in the evening's darkness. The trees still held drops from the last downpour and shook them off when the wind blew. My open buggy was no protection as my sodden trousers and jacket proved.

Betsy, my old horse, plodded along as tired as I, her head drooping like mine. She turned off the main road onto an almost-hidden one. Hidden if you didn't know where it was. That's the way Hank wanted it.

Along the right side was a breakfront of trees, all tall and sturdy. On my left, fields of grass and bushes, untilled and unowned. The road wasn't much more than a cow path with two deep ruts. But it had a promise of comfort at the end of it, closer than going home, that's what old Betsy was thinking and I didn't signal her otherwise.

Hank and his daughter, Mary, lived alone. He stopped going into town five years ago. Mary was the one who fetched what they needed. His sudden seclusion was talked about in town with various explanations—a man of mystery, someone with a hidden past. As many reasons given as there were people to speak them. Not that folk had a lot of time for gossiping, nor was Hank a person they gossiped most about.

I was the only one who saw him on a regular basis. Like this evening, coming back from seeing a patient.

Before the house came into sight, Betsy stopped. I must've been dozing. It took me a minute to take in the situation. We weren't at the house yet, so why did she stop? I reached to pick up the reins and that's when I saw a figure lying on the road. I immediately grabbed my bag and hopped down.

Young man, early twenties, I guessed. Bullet wound in his back, on the left side just above the belt line. Feeling the front of him, it looked like the bullet had passed through. He was sopping wet, ice cold, and was about as white as anybody can get. White, about to turn blue. How long had he lain there?

He was no lightweight but I finally got him into the buggy. I tucked a blanket around him, climbed on the seat, and urged Betsy forward. I hoped the wounds wouldn't open with the jostling on the rutted road.

The road ended at the house. One of the hunting dogs barked, but the other four just ran around the buggy and Betsy, their tails wagging.

Hank came out first, lantern held high, knowing it was me beforehand. When he saw another figure in the buggy, he half turned to his daughter and said, "Git back in the house, girl!"

"Help me with him, Hank, he's lost a lot of blood."

"I ain't havin' no stranger in my house."

"If you don't help me this minute, we're both going to be accused of murder."

"What!"

Even in the poor light I could see that hit him like a blow. I hadn't meant to say it quite that way. He hurriedly set the lantern on the porch and stumbled down the two steps in his haste. I thought together we'd get him into the house, but before I could move, Hank picked him up and carried him in. The strength of the man!

He called to Mary, told her what to do, but she was already ahead of him. A spare bedroom off the main room was where we went. I had slept there often.

First, he laid the boy on an old blanket on the floor, for he was muddy and bloody. The snowy white of the linens and colorful patchwork quilt kept their pristineness.

"Get something for bandages, Mary." I pulled up his shirt. The wounds weren't bleeding. Good. "Do you have something warm I can put on him?"

Mary set down the ewer she'd filled with hot water next to the basin on the marble-topped stand. I used a cloth to wipe around the wounds, taking care not to disturb nature's sealing.

She came back with some good soft cotton material and scissors. I set to bandaging him up. Hank came in, shooed her out and shut the door. He pulled off the boy's clothes, washing him as best he could, and rubbing his arms and legs with a coarse towel. I checked him thoroughly but the gunshot wound was the main part of it. He also had bruises, probably from falling off his horse.

We dressed him in a nightshirt, pulled stockings on his feet then lifted him onto the bed. I covered him with the sheet and quilt.

We worked in silence. Hank was a taciturn man, no nonsense, and knew what to do in these circumstances.

The boy's clothing consisted of a cambric shirt, brown corduroy trousers and good boots. Nothing in his pockets. I shrugged. Highway robbery came to mind. This stranger was luckier than the other two. They'd been shot in the back. Found dead.

Hank came back with a copper warming pan filled with embers, wrapped another towel around it and stuck it next to the boy's feet.

At the moment, that was all we could do for him. We left the door open.

"Come on, Doc, have a little stew," Mary said. "It's nice and hot." The table was set with steaming bowls and bread fresh out of the oven. She put down coffee for both of us as we went to the table. The smells set my mouth to watering.

"Found him down your road a bit," I said between mouthfuls and in answer to Hank's question.

Everything was so good. Much better than my bachelor's dinner any night. To survive, I knew just what homes to stop to eat at, where I could bed down for the night. Or where I just went in, did the patching up and got out as fast as possible.

Here was like the home I never had, as a boy or an adult, and as close as I'd get to having a family.

"Ever seen him before?" I asked them.

Hank's features were tight as though he was thinking of something sour. "You think he was coming here?"

"Doubt it. He probably just stumbled on the road and was following it." I knew it was what Hank wanted to hear. More'n likely it was true.

"How'd he get shot?" Hank's voice was gruff, not liking any of this. If he hadn't been eating such good food, he'd be growling.

"You know as much as I do," I said.

The rest of the meal we ate in silence. I checked my patient then joined Hank by the fire and lit my pipe. "His color is coming back."

"I've got some broth simmering. Is he awake yet?" said Mary.

I shook my head.

Didn't matter if it was a hurt sparrow or a hurt man, she was ready to take care of it. Knew she'd already been to the barn to see to Betsy. Probably the reason my old horse headed down the lane.

Since the boy had my usual place of repose, Hank gave me his bed and he put a bedroll for himself before the fire.

I got up a couple of times during the night to check on my patient. He hadn't moved but he was warming up and breathing normally. Ah, the recuperative powers of the young!

Hank was awake both times, sitting in his chair, pipe in his mouth, blue tin coffee cup in hand. He just nodded to me and went back to staring into the flames.   I knew how he felt about strangers and he wasn't taking too kindly to having one under his roof.

I slept much later than I expected to. Chalk it up to the thick curtains over the window that kept out the morning light. I hurriedly washed my face and combed my hair, looking at the old man who stared back at me from the oval, wood-framed mirror. The sun and wind had made their impressions on my face. Thinking of old made me think of my young patient.

Good smells of pancakes and maple syrup greeted me. Hank was where I'd seen him last. I guess he wasn't leaving the stranger alone in his house—with his daughter. That's the look that was on his face.

"He's been babbling a bit," said Mary. "He's taken a little broth." Her cheeks had a mite more color than usual. Another patient of hers on the mend.

Passing through the kitchen, I went in to see him. He was still lying flat. I took a look at his bandages. No blood. His eyes followed me as though I was the one who had shot him.

"I'm a Doc," I said. "Found you up the road a bit." I asked him a few questions about how he felt and was pleased with his answers.

"Why don't you tell me who you are and what happened," I said.

"My name's Johnny Bell," he answered. He looked at me, like that might mean something. "I was just riding through, looking for work. I heard the crack of the rifle, but that's all I remember. When I came to everything I had was gone—horse, gun, money. I started looking for a farm house. That's all I remember." He looked past me and I turned.

Hank stood in the doorway leaning in with his hands on either side of the door frame.

"Seems there's been a lot of highway robberies here of late," I said, speaking the truth. "Sounds like you were their pickins for the day."

"Maybe." He didn't sound too sure that I was right.

I asked Johnny a few more questions about how he came to be in this area, but got no better answers than the ones he'd first given me. I knew Hank wanted those questions asked, and how he wasn't satisfied with the answers, but there it was.

* * * *

When he was about recovered, almost a month later, he started helping Hank and Mary around the place a little. Hank still wanted him gone. Nothing to do with the manners of the boy for I could see he'd been brought up right and proper.

I got him out of there as soon as was reasonable. Fixed him up with a job in the hardware store. Clem Enderley who owned the store was laid up with a messy break of his left leg. He could still do a lot of things but he needed someone with two good legs.

Johnny worked out well. Clem took a shine to the boy. Seems most folks did. Hank would've too, under other circumstances.

Right from that first week in town, Johnny came with me out to Hank's place, always asking first if he could. Maybe not to see Hank especially, but he didn't show that it was for any other reason than to help them out a bit. Trying to repay them for their hospitality. He'd even bring out stuff from the store that he'd bought. Hank still wasn't too fond of having the boy around, number one, nor of him doing things on the farm, number two. Hank was still wary of him.

The boy had something on his mind, and I didn't have the foggiest idea as to what it was. There wasn't anything crooked about him and he wasn't a thief, but he was hiding something. He didn't just come to Los Olivos by chance.

I didn't want any of my friends getting hurt. Since I was the one who brought them all together, I wanted to follow up on my instincts. Since he came over to my cabin frequently in the evening, I had the opportunity to find out what he was up to, what his hidden past was.

He never drank too much so there was no way to get him drunk and talking. I figured I knew him as well as anyone so I asked him a few questions.

"Are you married?"

"No, sir," he said.

"Promised?"

"No, sir."

"Taken a shine to Mary, have you?"

"Well, sir, she's a very nice young lady."

"Yes, yes, but are you thinking about courting her, maybe setting up housekeeping?"

"Well, no," he said, and fidgeted about a bit, then he left early that night.

* * * *

A few days later, I'd checked on Clem and was walking from his house through the back of the hardware store. I overheard a strange voice talking to the boy.

"Ya gotta stake me. I ain't got money at all. Don't forget I can tell everybody who you are and why you're here."

The boy shushed him up real good so I couldn't hear anything else. He must have given him some money because the young hellion went out of the hardware store with a big grin on his face and smart-stepped across the street to the saloon without looking left or right. I slipped out the back door and I was almost in his tracks before he even got his boots out of them.

I stayed off, watching him. He drank continuously, got into a poker game and lost steadily.

Pretty soon he was out of money, out of the game and out of whiskey. He just sat there awhile playing with a copper coin, twirling it around and around on the empty table.

I could tell what was going through his mind. Maybe he could get some more from the boy, that's what he was thinking. I went to the bar, got us both whiskeys and carried them over to him. I sat down and began some idle conversation, then inched towards my real questions.

"I see you know Johnny."

"Johnny who?"

"Johnny Bell at the hardware store."

"That ain't...nah, don't know nobody in this town."

"What made you think it was this town I was talking about?"

"What...hey, what are you trying to pull, mister?"

"Look, don't get riled. I heard you talking to Johnny. I don't know what his real name is, but I guess you do."

He was now drunk, and not a good liar anyhow. Got out of him that they knew each other from a small town in Texas. Knew the boy had left a few months ago to go north to find the man who killed his pa and he was going to kill him in return.

"Who is this man your friend is going to kill?"

"Damned if I know, or care. I never knew where he got hisself off to. I jist drifted through town and ran into him. That's all I know, mister."

"Another drink?"

"Sure."

I could tell he was eyeing me to see if he could wheedle anything else out of me. Talked to him a little longer, but I believe that's all he really knew. I gave him some money, suggesting that he keep drifting and painted a little picture as to what would happen if he didn't. One town is just as good as another to a drifter.

At my place that night, over apple pie and coffee with the whisky bottle half full in between us, I told Johnny what his "friend" had revealed. Needless to say he was hopping mad. He tried to leave but I told him I'd just hang on his shirttail until he told me the truth about why he was in Los Olivos.

It took a while before he started his talking.

Johnny's mother had just died and in going through her things he found a letter she had stashed away. "The man who wrote that letter says he saw the gunfighter right here in Los Olivos. The one who killed my pa. The letter was five years old, but that's the only lead I have. That's why I'm here."

"And what are you going to do when you find him?"

"I'm going to shoot him down just like the dog he is. Just like he shot my pa."

"Tell me about it." I poured us another healthy shot of whiskey.

"I was four years old. Ma and me were on the boardwalk just coming out of the emporium when I saw my pa across the road. I was going to run to him when I saw him pull his gun, then all this blood is spurting out of him and he's falling down. I ran to him but he was already on the ground, dead."

"So you saw who shot him?"

"I don't remember. I was too busy watching my pa. Then my mother carried me off. Don't really remember much else. Ma never much talked about him even on a good day."

I took another sip of whiskey knowing that drinking the whole bottle in one gulp wasn't going to take the dread away. Wish I had a tonic for those things. The bigger problem at the moment was what to say to someone who has been planning an act of revenge for almost all his life and was closing in on his target?

"You have someone in mind?" I said.

He sat there quiet all through me fixing my pipe, staring off and seeing pictures in his mind. I kept glancing at him while I was tamping the tobacco down.

Finally I got it out of him. A whispered name I could barely hear. "Hank."

"Why him?" I said, trying not to get too riled up. "Why not Clem Enderly or Seth Barstow at the General Store for starters? A lot of other men in Los Olivos and a lot of others on farms around here."

"Not somebody who never comes to town like he doesn't want to be seen. Like he's hiding out. And if that's not enough, heard him talking to Mary when they thought I was sleeping. Something he said."

"You mean while you were delirious? Even if you're right, and I think you're plumb out of your head just like you were then, if you kill Hank or anyone, you're going to end up doing just what you think he's doing. Hiding out. Hiding the past. Hiding out and regretting your life."

"I gotta do this. After I read that letter, I swore on my mother's grave that I'd have revenge for Pa's death."

"Did she ask you to do this?"

"No. But she never married again and I always thought she was still longing for him."

"You don't know that. I'm not saying anything against your pa, but you don't know what went on between them. Maybe she had a bad experience and didn't want to repeat it. So don't say that you're doing this revenge for her. You're doing it for yourself. You just want an excuse to justify killing somebody. You're not even sure who it is. You better get some more proof, boy, since you're talking about my friend." I knew I was getting hepped up, but I just couldn't help it. I was harboring a viper in my bosom, namely this kid, and I was none too happy about it.

He made a move to get up, but I said, "Wait up a bit. I'm not finished yet. You say this man who shot your pa was a gunfighter. How do you know he can't beat you at the draw still? And, if you beat him, there'll be someone coming after you. Well, boy, let me tell you, there'll always be someone faster than you.

"Better to start mending fences. See if Mary will have you, settle down, do some good in the community."

* * * *

I could only hope he'd start forgetting about revenge, about taking someone else's life, so I taught him all I could about saving lives. Took him along with me calling on sick folk and letting him help me in my office when he could. He seemed ready enough to tag along and help, yet I had to believe he was still thinking about getting even for his father's murder. But he never let on that there was even a ghost of that thought in his mind.

I didn't press him on whether he was going to ask Mary the big question.

If he had his revenge, he wouldn't be getting Mary. Surely he knew that.

When I tore July off the calendar, I decided to bait him a little that evening, see which way he jumped on the issue. I wanted it resolved and the idea of revenge gone. "How can you be looking to kill a man," I said to him, "when you're helping me patch them up?"

"That man is different. He doesn't deserve to live." He hadn't paused a beat, knew exactly what I was talking about.

"Thought only God was supposed to be making decisions like that."

And speaking of God, I took him to church with me a couple of times, but he was too restless to be sitting still listening to the preacher talk about forgiveness.

He'd seem to forget his purpose for days on end. He had a real head for making people feel better, good bedside manner. I was right proud of him. Then I'd catch him with that look in his eyes. Seemed like he was going back and forth. Not wanting to give up on his mission of revenge, but liking what he was doing with sick and ailing folks, seeing them get better because of what he was doing for them.

I told him people make mistakes, bad ones, but they have to go on, and getting revenge was not the way to do that.

"Hank's a good man," I said. "Been working that farm for a lotta years. Got married along the way, had Mary, but her mother died in childbirth. Me and Hank raised Mary between us. So it's not every young fellow I'd be suggesting to ask for Mary's hand. She's almost as much my daughter, too."

A father is a father, right or wrong. And the kid had seen his father shot down. Had to take that into account as to how Johnny felt.

Johnny couldn't forget that day when he was four years old. And neither could I.

That day was the turning point in our lives for Hank and me. I took to remembering—

* * * *

"Hey, you."

Hank and I were in a small town in Texas, crossing the dusty road that ran through its center. Had a boardwalk that was covered over on the other side. It being mighty hot in Texas in the summer, we were headed for the shade.

We turned around at the voice. In the middle of the road was a man about twenty, if that. His eyes were on me. Seen that look before, lots of times. Knew what he wanted, but I wasn't going to give it to him. Hank looked at me. We turned around and kept walking toward the shade.

A bullet hit the dust near me, sending up a little cloud. Hank threw himself down. I turned, after all it was me he had his sights on. I made no move for my gun. Knew he wasn't going to shoot me outright. That's not what he wanted.

"What can I do for you, mister?" I said, slow and easy-like trying not to rile him further.

"Want to see just how fast you are."

"Guess I'm just fast enough to still be alive. We're just passing through, not looking for any trouble."

"No trouble. Thought we could draw and see who wins."

"Why?"

"Because I think I'm faster than you."

"I agree with you. You're faster than me."

"We gotta prove it, lest folks don't believe me."

I bet a lotta of folks didn't believe anything he said. He *had* to prove it. I didn't doubt he was fast. Typical small town kid who'd outgunned anybody who'd challenged him and now he wanted to go up against the big guys. I sighed. There are no old, bold gunfighters.

"We're in town on business, maybe you can help us. There's some gold in it for you." Hoped the thought of money might change his mind. "Any strangers in town?" We were bounty hunting, a good job for fast guns.

The mention of gold didn't change his look by even a flicker of his eyes. He wasn't interested, at least not at this minute. Maybe later, when he shot somebody and wanted to buy drinks on the house. Probably at the same saloon he'd just come out of.

"Draw first and we'll talk later." He was still holding his gun on me. "I'm putting up my gun. Get ready to go at it." He slid the gun into his holster, his hand hovering over it.

"Let's talk first and if you're still of a mind for drawing then we'll settle the matter about that. There's a nice reward for this fellow."

By this time the whole town knew our business, not that they didn't size us up the minute we rode in. Problem with them all knowing was that the man we were hunting knew also and was probably saddling up at the livery stable that very moment.

"Draw!" he shouted.

"I'm not drawing." I turned my back and started walking toward the shade. I heard the sound of the gun slide the leather. I dove for the dust as a bullet whizzed past my head. Another shot sounded at the same time so they could have been as one.

Which meant they weren't from the same gun.

As I rolled over, the man was starting to crumple, his chest red. Hank was still in the prone position only now with his gun out.

Before I could move, a four-year old boy ran over yelling "Pa, Pa," and threw himself over the red chest.

Something gripped my heart with a spiked fist. I couldn't move, only watch the scene play out.

The boy was followed by a woman who was barely out of girlhood. She stood looking down at the man, her eyes a lot older than the rest of her, then pulled the boy, now bloodied, off his father.

The way I remembered the woman looking down on her husband, she wasn't feeling too sorry, like maybe she expected him to come to this end, like maybe she was even hoping for it. Maybe I read a lot into that look that might'n have been there. But that's what I saw.

From that day, we gave up bounty hunting. I swore I'd help people live and use all I'd learned in the Army to be the best doctor I could. Hank took to farming.

Hank saved my life and I never forgot that.

He never forgot the boy who saw his father killed.

There were some things I couldn't heal.

* * * *

Then things happened all at once. It was Sunday afternoon when everybody should be taking things easy. The boy wasn't. I saw him take off with a look on his face that sure gave me a bad feeling. He was headed for Hank's place and he didn't look like he was going acourtin'. The buggy would be too slow so I borrowed a horse at the livery stable and took off after him.

By the time I got there he had a gun on Hank. They stood on the porch. No dogs around so they must be with Mary in the barn or someplace.

"Wait," I yelled, and jumped off the horse as fast as I could. I kept my hands up away from my gun, but I had on a long coat so there wasn't any way I could get to it fast anyhow. "What's going on here?"

"I've found the killer of my father."

"You must have just heard something. What was it?"

"Heard that Hank here used to be a gunfighter."

"That so." I was on the porch now. "So what are you going to do?"

"Shoot him. Like he did my pa."

"You mean, you're going to outdraw him?"

"He didn't give my pa that chance, so I'm not going to give him the chance either."

I realized that was his reasoning all along, not that it mattered now. He was scared, the gun shaking.

"Let's back up a minute. Hank here didn't kill your father."

His eyes glanced over at me. If Hank had wanted to, he could have shot him in that moment. But he didn't.

"Yeah. Then who did?" He glanced back at Hank.

I stepped between them.

"I did."

"No. You're just trying to save his life. He's no good...." But he couldn't go on, couldn't see too well with the tears in his eyes.

"I'm going to tell you the truth, but you're not going to believe me. Your daddy drew first. He was fast. I dropped to the ground so he missed and I got a shot off. Hit him square in the chest."

I could hear Hank behind me making noises like he wanted to say something.

"My Pappy drew first?"

"Like I said, he was fast. Wasn't expecting me to drop out of the line of fire like I did."

The boy looked dazed. "You?" he said. He looked over my shoulder at Hank but his gaze was sightless.

I didn't say anything. Wasn't sure how this was going to play out. But I knew I was plumb worn out waiting for this thing the kid had for revenge to come to a head. When a wound is festering, you've got to squeeze all the poison out.

"If you're going to shoot somebody it's got to be me." I stood there waiting for him to decide, something he'd been in a tizzy about all along.

"You didn't do anything before because you didn't have the proof. Now you have it. You're either going to shoot me and give up doctoring—because you can't go on with learning about that if you're ready to kill somebody. And you're not going to be wedding Mary because you're going to be on the run from the sheriff. He'll be after you before your gun gets cold. Probably sic some bounty hunters on you."

The boy's eyes looked into mine as though he wanted to see right into my brain and know what I was thinking. I stared him right back and hoped he couldn't read my thoughts.

"See that's what we were doing that day, looking for a man who'd shot somebody. Gotta tell you the sheriff from your town was there and he saw what happened. He didn't lock either of us up, just told us to keep on moving. Which we did. Never did get the guy we were after."

I was talking slow and soft keeping my hands in sight, standing as still as I could. The boy's eyes wavered. He wasn't looking at Hank over my shoulder anymore. He was just sort of looking past him. Like he didn't know what to do.

I was so close I could have grabbed his gun, but that wouldn't make any decisions for him. This had to be resolved. He had to decide he was going to avenge his father's death, or think about his own life and what he was going to do with it.

There was a call from the barn. Mary. Johnny turned, distracted. I could've grabbed his gun or could've pulled mine out. Maybe that's what he wanted. But I didn't.

Mary didn't seem to notice the gun in his hand or the way we were standing with me in front of Hank.

He stood there, watching Mary walk toward us, the dogs dancing around her, running forward to us then back to her, like she was some sort of fairy princess, who had power over all the animals.

If she guessed something was wrong, she didn't let on, but she did have a puzzled look on her face. "Are you staying to dinner, Doc? Johnny?"

The boy tried to say something to her, but it was only a strangled sound. Then he jumped off the porch, ran to his horse, hopped on and galloped off. Think he still had his gun in his hand.

Mary looked at us for an explanation. I just greeted her like it was any other day. She looked at us both and went into the house.

I stepped away from Hank.

I heard Hank uncock his gun. So he had drawn.

"Why'd you do that?" he said.

"You saved my life, seemed only fair I return the favor."

"He might have shot you."

"Wasn't really sure what he was going to do."

"Not too many friends like you around," Hank said.

"I thought the same thing that day." I nodded in the direction Johnny had taken. "Guess you'll be coming to town a little more often now that there's nothing to hide from."

"Maybe I will, and maybe I won't." He opened the door for me. "Come on in for dinner, unless your cooking suddenly got as good as your bravery."

♦ ♦ ♦

Gay Toltl Kinman has nine award nominations for her writing; several short stories in American and English magazines and anthologies; six children's books; a Y.A. gothic novel; two adult mysteries; several short plays produced; articles in professional journals and newspapers; and co-edited two non-fiction books. Kinman has library and law degrees.

Raiatea

Molly Rae Doust

Raiatea sat on her rock where the reef rose from the surf line. She held her ukulele against her royal blue scales and strummed with smooth, strong fingers. Long, dark hair fell over the strings, but she didn't care. Her ululating voice carried over the waves to the shore where lonely, despondent men lifted their heads like hounds on the scent.

* * * *

John Babcock sweated. He loosened his collar but that didn't help. He still sweated, finding breathing a difficult task. He tossed back the second rum and glanced around to see who else was in the pub at 10 in the morning. Not too many customers. Even the barkeep paid him no mind. That was good. Maybe they hadn't caught on.

It had seemed easy, innocent at first. The amounts. And for Pete's sake, it's not like it was for a charity or something. It was a pirate ship! John had signed on to the *Elegant* in Portsmouth. He knew next to nothing about crewing a sailing ship, but there you go. They took him and he was grateful. Later, months later, when he'd been more or less accepted as one of them, he'd seen how easy it would be.

It started after a particularly well-endowed English Navy ship fell into their trap. At first John believed Captain Smits who said they were "keeping it safe for them" when he asked about the bullion. Sure, he'd been gullible, but again, what did he know about navy ships and merchant vessels? He'd had a bit too much rum that night, and when he awoke to cannon fire and rushed on deck, the Captain had said the other ship was on fire and they needed to help. He'd squinted across the gap but saw no flames. He *had* had a lot to drink.

The *Elegant* moved parallel to the Navy ship and closed the gap. Men swung between the ships and the Navy returned fire. They didn't seem to want help. Perhaps they didn't realize their danger? Flames broke out and in the glow, John saw fighting. The *Elegant*'s crew began moving chests from the Navy ship onto theirs.

Finally the Navy crew realized their danger as the ship listed. They tossed out life boats and dropped into them.

Hours later, after John sobered up, he thought perhaps the Captain's claim that they were 'pre-eminent nautical salvage engineers' was over stated. That made it easier to rationalize his own stealing, the reason he'd joined the crew in the first place. He couldn't seem to resist helping himself to other people's money. However, in Portsmouth, it had caught up with him, just like it seemed to have now.

"Another," he called to the barkeep. More rum slopped into his glass. He'd really have to change his ways, but how? His first task was to avoid capture and probable death from Captain Smits and his crew. Then, to get back to the various ports where he'd hidden his stolen money. He hadn't kept it on the ship, they would have found it and he'd have been sliced open and fed to the sharks.

* * * *

Raiatea stopped strumming. The uke lay in her wet lap as she inhaled deeply. She smelled one. She smelled a perfect choice. She would hear him soon, but that he was near was enough. She would see him when it was far too late for him to save himself. That was her job. Saving. She smiled, her slightly pointed teeth glinting in the morning sun. She swam toward the wharf, the cluster of buildings beyond it, holding her choice.

* * * *

John definitely had too much rum on an empty stomach. He started to feel exposed in the pub as more patrons entered. He paid his bill and wobbled to the alley entrance.

He leaned against the wall and peered up and down. Seemed safe, so he continued toward the wharf in hopes of finding something to eat from a vendor and a new ship out of town. The wharf was relatively calm and empty, the early rush of fish mongers long gone and no new ships in port yet. He eyed the *Elegant* far down the quay. All quiet. However, the crew would wake soon from wherever they had spent the night and return to the ship. He didn't have long. He heard a high note of music wafting to him on the breeze. He stopped and listened. A bird? An animal? Too high and too sustained he thought, for a person. A musical instrument. He nodded to himself and ambled toward it. Why not? It was in the opposite direction from the *Elegant*. If it was a musician, vendors might be listening there, and he could eat.

* * * *

Raiatea reached the wharf and swam parallel until it met the main dock. The pilings were high above her, so she turned south until she reached the beach. She found a nice rock suited to her purpose, in the shallows where she could hide her tail. She pulled her ukulele from around her back where she'd hung it for swimming, and began to play, accompanying herself with her high noted song. She held a note for a ridiculously long time and then stopped and smelled. It was working. He was coming. She started her song again and held the note, until the man she waited for descended the rickety stairs from the dock to the beach and approached.

"I didn't know anyone could sing like that!" he said.

"I can."

"I mean, you can hold that note forever."

"Thank you."

"How do you breathe?" John took in the lovely, scantily clad woman sitting on a rock in the surf. Her royal blue dress trailed into the water. The upper part was sort of skin-colored, but hidden by thick, wet hair. She held a little guitar in her slim hands.

"Why doesn't your guitar get ruined in the water?" he asked.

"This is an ukulele. I got it on my travels." She strummed some lovely notes. "I use kelp resin as waterproofing. It's never ruined in the water. I can even play it under water. Would you like to hear it?"

"Yes, that sounds interesting."

She bent over and strummed just beneath the surface. It was lovely, but his attention was drawn by the flesh colored NOT dress.

"You're not from around here, are you?" he asked.

"No. Just visiting. I travel a lot."

"Me, too. In fact, I'm looking for my next ship. Adventure. Job."

"What do you do?"

"Pre-eminent nautical salvage engineer?"

"Ha. Pirate." She smelled victory.

"Yes. Well." He heard a ruckus coming from the dock. Were they coming for him? Best not to take chances.

"I guess I'd better be going."

"What's the rush?"

"My, uh, colleagues might not be too happy to see me."

"Don't you mean, you don't want to see them?"

John began to sweat again, the lovely music and visual display taking second to the picture of him drawn and quartered. "Yes, if you want to be exact."

"Oh, I do. I like exact. You should come with me."

"Where are you going?"

"Does it matter? As long as it's not here, right?"

"That's true." She held out her hand. He stepped into the water to help her from the rock, but she was very strong. He was yanked into the surf and dragged out past the end of the pier before he could take a breath. In fact, he found he was breathing, sort of, as the shore receded. He wasn't even swimming, although he moved very fast through the water. Must be the rum.

After several minutes and who knows how far in distance, she slowed and let go of his hand. He immediately began to sink.

"You can't swim?" she asked.

"Arghlrk," he said.

"Great. That's going to make it harder." She hauled him up.

He could not see land anywhere. His heart raced and he kicked his legs reflexively.

"What's going on?" he gurgled.

"We can help each other."

"How can I help you in the middle of the ocean?" He really took in his surroundings. "The middle of the ocean. How much rum did I have?"

"I don't know, but not that much. You're safe now."

"Safe? I can't swim and the sea is far from safe. Sharks, among other things."

"Don't worry. This is my home. I'll keep you safe."

"Yeah. About that. I see your tail. I know what you are. I know what you do. You're a mermaid and you take hapless sailors out to sea and drown them. And eat them. Or something. I was never clear on the rest."

Raiatea laughed. "That is so funny. I'm not going to drown you. I told you, you can help me."

"Are you going to keep me as your human husband? To do your bidding no matter how unsavory?" he asked a little hopefully.

"It's early days to discuss marriage, but I'm not opposed on principal."

"I'm getting cold."

"I forgot. You're not used to this." She took off swimming again, her powerful tail propelling them both. She drew up to a deserted beach warm in the afternoon sun.

"Better?" she asked.

"Much. I'm hungry."

"It's always something with you humans." She disappeared and reappeared with a fish. "Here, eat."

"It's raw."

"Baby. Like this." She took a bite and handed him the fish.

"Sheesh. If we're supposed to help each other, we're going to work out some food issues." He took a small bite. It was fresh-tasting and not fishy at all. "This is delicious!"

"I know. Let's get down to business."

John gnawed on his raw fish.

"I am not *that* kind of mermaid. We are helper mermaids. Our race and culture stipulate that we have to help humans, not destroy them."

"Right. Why haven't I heard of you?"

"We keep a low profile. Oh, there is the *other* kind of mermaid, but they like to be known and feared. Us, not so much."

John pondered this as he ate. "So what do you want from me?"

"You are a perfect subject. You have made some not very good choices in your life and it's gotten you into trouble, correct?"

"It didn't used to."

"Stop pouting. We mermaids have special abilities and I can make this all go away. You'd like that, wouldn't you?"

"No more running? No more people trying to kill me?"

"Well, not for the reasons they are now."

"What's that supposed to mean?"

"Just be sure that your career as a pirate would be over, and no former "colleagues" would try to kill you. Good enough?"

"What do I have to do?"

"Part of our deal is that you follow my instructions. I can change your past, and in effect, your future. You'd be safe."

"Fine. But what do I have to *do*?"

"Nothing, really. You're helping me out by letting me change your life. It's my duty. My calling. It's what I do."

"What if I say no?"

"Nothing. Your life goes on as before. Sought after, always on the run, perhaps hung from the highest yardarm in your future. I go on looking for someone else to help and fulfill my cultural and mermatarian duty."

John finished the fish. Well, all the parts he decided were food. He considered her offer. He was tired of running. He knew someone somewhere would eventually catch up to him. Maybe she could even help him recover his treasures from all the places he'd hidden it. She could swim them both there faster than a ship. He could offer to share it with her. After he'd recovered it, of course. He thought of something.

"I just thought of something. I won't forget my past, will I? Where I'm from, who my family is?"

"Of course not. Just these ugly bits will no longer be a problem for you. Also, you won't feel the compulsion to steal anymore. Or to commit crimes. You'll be an excellent citizen, which is our goal. To make the world a better place, one human at a time."

"What happens to me? Am I trapped here forever in the ocean? Or on this tiny island with no pub?"

"No, silly. Once we have our agreement, I will take you wherever you want to go."

"No strings?"

"Strings? Ukulele?"

"No. I mean, no other conditions or rules?"

"No. That's it."

"Will I ever see you again?"

"That is unlikely."

John rose and washed his hands at the water's edge. He really had nothing to lose. His enemies would be instantly gone, and not because he'd had them killed. They would simply forget about him. Freedom. Traveling the world as a man of leisure. Idyllic.

"Okay. I agree."

Raiatea pulled an agreement written on sea weed from some hidden crevice. "Sign here."

He checked the agreement and saw exactly what she had said. He signed with the quill she handed him. Black ink. He raised an inquiring eye brow.

"Octopus," she said.

Figured. "All done. As to where I want to go, I have a map." He pulled his oil skin map from his own hidden crevice and showed her where he hidden the first cache.

"What's this?" she asked.

"My treasure map. Where I hid my spoils." He chuckled.

"What spoils?"

"You know, my uh, borrowing."

"That doesn't exist."

"What do you mean?"

"Well, I said I'd erase your past so your enemies couldn't find you. That means you haven't stolen anything. They have no reason to hunt you."

"What?" John sat with a thump on the sand. All his dreams ran through his head and out into the blue. All gone. Just like that. He flopped back onto the sand.

"Well, now that you're a better person, where do you want me to drop you?"

"It doesn't matter. Portsmouth, I guess." Years of hard work stealing, gone just like that. He'd probably have to get a real job. A merchant or something. It sounded awful. The other part of what she'd said was true; he had no desire to steal again. It was too much work.

Raiatea tucked the map into her hidden crevice, took his hand and entered the water. John barely remembered the swim to Portsmouth. The water grew even colder, but that didn't matter. She left him on the sand near the wharf.

Raiatea swam out to a rock above the surf line and pulled out his map. "Very nice. I should be able to recover most of this within a few days." She was an excellent swimmer. It was amazing how they all believed their lives were changed. How they *wanted* their lives to change. That was why she preferred white collar criminals; more profitable. She swam off to find her fortune. Well, *his* fortune.

◆ ◆ ◆ ◆

Molly Rae Doust has written a few short stories. She only comes out of her box on full moons in between raising kids, tending her husband and corralling the cats and dogs.

Dago Red

Margaret Searles

Margaret Millet enjoyed her weekend job at Gambol Mini-Storage—right up until the Sunday morning when Socrates, the elderly black Labrador guard dog, sniffed and barked and snuffed and woofed at the roll-up door of a storage unit in Building E. That morning all the fun went out of the job.

The locker should have been vacant and openable, but it was padlocked instead. What in the world was Soc going on about? Mrs. Millet put her own nose close to the door and got a whiff of something acrid and pungent.

She shook her cropped gray and beige head and hustled her well-filled blue jeans back to the office. That unit should have been empty; Mrs. Millet had processed the "vacate" herself. The tenant had been in the process of clearing it out when she left work, the night before.

Yes, that was locker E8 all right. The green "vacancy" pin glared from the wall chart and the tenant's file card said "out 8/27." Did he fail to finish emptying it? Or did something else happen? Why was it padlocked and *what* was inside?

She looked back from the office doorway. Soc had not budged from Building E, Unit 8. Scrunched flat on the asphalt, nose to the bottom of the door, she whined anxiously. Her whole demeanor said, "Something wrong here—bad news. Open up—gotta check this out!" Then the dog hoisted her tubby body up on her stiff old legs and woofed sharply, hackles raised. "Aren't you going to do something about this? I'm telling you, it smells bad!"

Mrs. Millet eyed the gate. Nobody. She was quite alone, except for the dog. "Okay, old girl. Yes, I'm it. I'll do something."

The night watchman was long gone to wherever he went in the daytime. Why hadn't Socrates handed him this problem? He lived in the apartment over the office and did more sleeping than watching, but he was supposed to leave Soc out at night and respond if she barked.

Mrs. Millet called the locker's ex-renter, one Phillip Sand. He said, "I was out right after you left. I rolled down the door like you told me and kept my padlock. No, I've no idea why it's locked now. Sorry..."

He seemed neither surprised nor curious. Sand was new in town and had only used the locker for a couple of weeks, while he looked for an apartment. When he found one, he'd asked for a partial refund on his rent. He'd been nosy, too—asked a lot of questions and wandered among the storage buildings, talking to the other renters he came across. Well, at least he had not met with foul play.

What, then? Kids playing pranks? The homeless who often camped outside the fence, dumping their garbage?

She called her emergency numbers next—the Manager, then the owners—and reached no one. Were they all out of town? Well, she'd have to check it out herself. She picked up the stout bolt cutters, part of the storage facility's standard equipment.

Oh, Good! Here was Mr. Geranium, her favorite customer, just driving in the gate. She told him all about it and said, "I want a witness. There could be drugs or something worse in there. Socrates doesn't fuss over trifles."

"Of course. Here, let me." Mr. Geranium shouldered the bolt cutters with an understanding smile on his lean, aristocratic face. They left Soc in the office, and Mr. Geranium cut off the padlock and rolled up the locker door.

The potent smell that had so dithered Socrates billowed out, and Mrs. Millet stared in disbelieving horror. The body of a man lay slumped in the back corner of the locker, limbs at odd angles, the upturned face dirty and unshaven, slack and empty of life. His filthy hair was the color of carrots. By the smell and the condition of his head and ragged overcoat, wine had been poured all over him. Two large, empty bottles, labeled the cheapest kind of red wine, stood upright by his feet like candlesticks at a wake.

Mr. Geranium peered over her shoulder, then stumbled back and blurted, "*Dago Red*?"

"What?" His words gave Mrs. Millet the power to move, and she turned to him, shocked all over again to see him so pale and shaken. A veteran of World War Two, and he looked as queasy as she felt.

"Er, sorry, no offense—it's the wine. Used to call that stuff Dago Red," he mumbled. "Do you know him?"

"No," Mrs. Millet said, reluctantly taking a closer look. "He might have come over the fence? Part of the homeless camp along the creek. They get water from our faucet sometimes. We find the hose unscrewed."

Mrs. Millet called 911 and the place soon swarmed with police. Customers showed up, as well, and came to the office to ask what had happened.

Mr. Geranium stood in the doorway and held Soc so she wouldn't bolt back to the crime scene. Mrs. Millet started her electric kettle and made tea. She handed Mr. Geranium a hot mug-full and went back behind the counter, letting him fend off the curious. One customer wailed, "Imagine—I'll never come here after hours again! Was he murdered, do you know?" Mrs. Millet didn't listen to Mr. Geranium's answer; watching him give it was enough. He bent his gray head deferentially, aloof and cool. Only too shocking, but no harm could possibly come to a good person like yourself, Madam... Whatever his words, this was the message imparted.

How lucky he had come along! Mrs. Millet only knew him as a customer, but most weekends he turned up at least once, stopping in the office to chat and often bringing lemons or avocados from his trees or tomatoes from his garden. He used his storage space for items he bought and sold at local swap meets. Mrs. Millet wondered if he depended on this trade for income, but she had never asked.

Mr. Geranium was a widower, he said, and quite alone in the world. Mrs. Millet was single (long divorced) herself, and wished he'd be even more friendly—ask her to dinner, for instance. With another sort of man, she might have asked him, but something about Mr. Geranium said, "come this far and no farther." A mystery man, her friend Judy Hark called him, and sometimes asked, "How are things with your Mystery Man?"

Judy Hark. Suddenly in need of her friend's support and comfort, Mrs. Millet reached for the telephone. "Judy? Yes, I'm at work. Are you sitting down? Good. We found a dead body in a locker this morning..."

When she finished, Judy said, "Margaret, you never should have taken that job. I said so at the time—and now look what you've got yourself mixed up in!" Hardly the support and comfort Mrs. Millet sought.

"You know I need the money, with my rentals vacant up in Oregon and the property taxes coming due—I never would have taken it otherwise. And I'm not mixed up in anything. It's nothing to do with me, except that I work here."

"Uh-huh. And see that it stays that way, is my advice. Let Chief Belgrave do this one by himself. Do you want me to come down? Can I bring you anything? You sound..."

Ah, that was more like her sympathetic friend. "Well, I am, a little... It's not every day a body turns up in the workplace. Mr. Geranium's here, and the police, and some customers..." Her voice trailed off weakly. It really was too much. She felt quite dizzy and overwhelmed.

"Sugar!" Mrs. Hark said. "Eat something sweet; you've had a shock. I'll be there in fifteen minutes."

The phone abruptly went dead and Mrs. Millet cradled the receiver, ashamed of imposing on her friend and at the same time glad and relieved that Judy was coming. Judy Hark was a rock in time of trouble. Their friendship went back many years, a curiosity in a way, since their lifestyles were totally different. Mrs. Millet lived in a converted garage behind her daughter's modest home, constantly struggled to make ends meet and avoided social affairs, while Judy, whose husband Willy had retired from a prosperous construction business, had a fine home, chaired committees and knew everybody in town.

A man in a tweed jacket with bulging patch pockets elbowed past Mr. Geranium and came up to the counter. He pulled out a small spiral notebook and said, "Mrs. Millet? Clovis Jones, Homicide. You found the victim, I understand. A few questions?"

For several minutes Mrs. Millet answered queries about the locker's renter, Phillip Sand, and the operation of Gambol Storage. She only declined to answer when he asked her age. "Mature," she said. The detective grinned and didn't press.

He laid a plastic bag on the counter. "This was all we found on the victim. Ever see it before?" The bag contained a gold pen, the kind filled from a bottle of ink. A beautiful pen, engraved with a cluster of grapes and initials in script so fancy she had never been sure what the letters were. Mrs. Millet had seen it, or one just like it, once each month—when Mr. Geranium wrote the check for his locker rent.

"I... I think so, yes."

She raised her eyes and met a look from Mr. Geranium that froze her vocal cords. The glare lasted only an instant. Then he released Socrates and approached the counter. "Yes, I see," he said, eyeing the plastic bag. "It's a lot like mine, isn't it?"

He produced his pen. Mrs. Millet was so relieved she laughed out loud. "Oh my, they are alike! As the old lady said about the Model A, 'I guess they made more than one!'"

The detective studied Mr. Geranium's pen and the one in the bag. "What are the initials?" he asked.

Before Mr. Geranium could answer, Judy Hark tacked through the office door, circumnavigated the two men and the counter, and put her arm around Mrs. Millet's shoulder. She must have left home immediately after Mrs. Millet's call, but looked elegant as always in a turquoise outfit that set off her auburn hair. "Hello, Mr. Geranium." She turned to look Clovis Jones in the eye. "What's this, the third degree?"

The detective flourished his notebook. "Who are you, Ma'am—and what's your connection with this matter?"

Horrified, Mrs. Millet said, "Oh, no, Officer! She's Judy Hark, my friend. I called her and she came, that's all."

Clovis Jones took Mrs. Hark's name, address, and telephone number, all the same. By the time he got back to the previous question, Mr. Geranium answered, cool as you please, "The pen, mine at least, was some sort of sales promotion. A winery—I forget the name. It was a good pen, so I kept it."

"And the initials? Are they yours?"

"Oh, no—the winery's logo, I guess." He dismissed the initials with a wave of his hand.

Pretty convincing, Mrs. Millet thought. No details, nothing elaborate, difficult to check, and vague enough to be true—but not the story he had told her. She opened her mouth and then closed it again. After all, his pen had not been found on the body.

Mrs. Hark said, "This has been a shock for Margaret. I'm sure she's happy to help, but she's had about enough, don't you think?"

The detective pocketed his notebook and said, "Okay, that's all for now. We may need to talk to you folks again later."

Mrs. Hark smiled sweetly and asked, "How did the poor man die, Lieutenant?"

"Blissfully drunk, I'd say," said Clovis Jones.

* * * *

"They've identified the body Margaret found," Willy announced from behind the morning paper. "Fingerprints. Says here he was a war hero in WW Two."

"Let's see." Mrs. Hark took the paper from her husband's hands and looked where he pointed. "The body found in a local storage locker has been identified as Joseph Rossi, of Trenton, New Jersey. He served in Italy during World War II, winning the DSM and Purple Heart. Police ask anyone with information to come forward."

A small, grainy picture of a young man in army uniform bisected the article at this point. He could have been any 1940s soldier. The picture had been cropped from a larger photo; Mrs. Hark could make out elbows and shoulders on either side of the subject.

The article continued: "'Definitely homicide,' said Chief Marion Belgrave, Gambol Beach Police. Autopsy showed the cause of death to be a stab wound to the heart. See MURDER, A8."

On page A8, a flash photo of the open locker showed a dark lump, presumably the body, in one corner. The wine bottles had caught the flash and glared out of the picture like a pair of headlights. Beneath this photo, the reporter had let himself go, suggesting everything from human sacrifice to a Mafia killing.

"This reporter wants a job with the tabloids! I'm surprised at the *Lighthouse-Courier*, printing this garbage."

Mrs. Hark gave the paper back to Willy, who settled his bulk deeper into his recliner and said, "You and Margaret aren't going to get into this, are you?"

"I don't know. Margaret says not, but they found a pen on the body, and Mr. Geranium—her Mystery Man you know—has one just like it. By the way, I'm meeting her for lunch today. Yours is in the fridge."

* * * *

A stiff sea breeze swept the patio at Shelley's Restaurant, so they took a table inside. Mrs. Hark ordered her usual half-sandwich and chowder, but Mrs. Millet failed to resist the chicken enchilada.

"Did you see the paper this morning?" Mrs. Hark asked.

"And the picture. Judy, I'd bet my next pay check that one of the soldiers cut off of that picture was Mr. Geranium." Mrs. Millet's tone was grave. "He was in Italy during the war, too. And those pens—he told the detective his was from a winery, but that's not the story he told me."

"Really?" Mrs. Hark lowered her voice to a whisper. "Why, Margaret, you don't think Mr. Geranium killed that man?"

Margaret whispered too. "I don't. He's such a kind, decent person. It's too fantastic to even think of... but... well, I'll tell you about his pen. I admired it one day, and he said an army buddy gave it to him, to commemorate a very tough spot they were in together, in Italy, during the war. Of course I asked for more, but he said it wasn't his story to tell."

"And here you find a body, and it's a man with an identical pen in his pocket! Margaret, why didn't you tell that detective?"

"Because it wasn't Mr. Geranium's pen."

"But the dead man served in Italy, too—there must be a connection! You should tell the police right away." Mrs. Hark put a lot of feeling into her whisper.

"Maybe I should. And another thing, that locker was the first vacant unit we've had in weeks. How did the killer know about it? And how did he get past the guard dog?"

"Oh, do call the police, Margaret." Mrs. Hark took a spoonful of chowder but scarcely noticed how tasty it was.

"Not until I see Mr. Geranium. If he knew the man, he should tell them. I know where he lives. Will you go with me?"

"Eat your lunch, and let me think about that," Mrs. Hark said.

* * * *

Mr. Geranium dwelt in a dubious neighborhood, his yellow frame house sheltered by lemon and avocado trees. The shrubs were clipped, and a pot of scarlet geraniums—his name sign?—glowed on the front stoop.

"As neat as if he was Navy," said Mrs. Millet, who had always been partial to the maritime branch.

"I hope it's safe to leave your truck on this street," Mrs. Hark said. She rapped sharply on the security screen (the place was covered like a fortress) and waited. Ah, here he was, unlocking deadbolts, swinging the front door in and peering through the perforated metal screen.

"Well, hello, Mrs. Hark! And Mrs. Millet—come in ladies, come in!" He pushed open the screen with a wide, astonished smile.

"We haven't time," Mrs. Millet said. "We're on our way to the police station."

Mr. Geranium joined them on the stoop, where three made a crowd. "Why is that?" he asked. "Has something else happened?"

"I gave her some advice." Mrs. Hark didn't budge an inch. "Margaret should have told them about your ink pen."

Looking up into his face, Mrs. Millet said, "I thought you might like to tell them yourself."

"A civic conscience; I might have known." Mr. Geranium's shoulders sagged, and he suddenly looked *old*. "I wish... Look, come in, and I'll tell you about that pen. Then if you really think the police need to know, I will go with you." He held the screen open.

Mrs. Hark said, "Fair enough," and a nursery jingle ran through her mind: "Won't you come into my parlor, said the spider to the fly; It's the prettiest little parlor...".

Mr. Geranium's parlor was like a cabin, dim and cozy, with knotty pine wainscoting, tweed carpet, and cushioned furniture. He ushered them to the sofa and sat in a wing chair opposite.

"I need to arrange my thoughts," he said. "Makes me wish I still smoked a pipe."

"Please don't," Mrs. Millet said without specifying pipe smoking or thought arrangement. "Just tell us about the pen. The dead man has been identified, you know. It's in this morning's paper."

"Has he! Very efficient, our police. Poor old Dago Red." Mr. Geranium's eyes were sad and far away as he added, "It was all so long ago."

"Dago Red! But you said that was the wine..."

"Oh, both. Both. Joe Rossi was a red-headed Italian, and in those days—remember, this was before political correctness—everybody called him Dago Red. But about the pen. Red had the pens engraved and gave them to us three years after the war. The initials on the pens are D R for Dago Red, the wine—and a certain incident." Mr. Geranium picked up his pen from a small table and handed it to Mrs. Hark.

"Not a winery promotion, then," Mrs. Millet said.

"There's a winery in the story, but not a promotion, no." He rose, paced across the room and back, then perched on the arm of his chair.

"There were five of us. We all had a year or two of college before being drafted, so they sent us to Oklahoma A & M, for officers' training. Two months later, they decided they didn't need officers and dumped the lot of us into the infantry. Saunders, Johnson, Lang, Rossi, and me—we all wound up in the same outfit, just in time for the invasion of Italy.

"We captured a little village in the mountains. The town had a winery, and some of us found a cave where they stored the wine. Well, soldiers and the spoils of war, you know.

"But we had bad luck. Our sergeant was a mean, ignorant bully, and he really had it in for us college boys. We used to call him Sergeant de Sade. Well, he found us in the cave. We were all pretty drunk, and someone hit him with a bottle—and he died. We were scared silly, as you can imagine, and we just left him there and sneaked back to camp.

"The next morning a German unit counter-attacked and pushed us off the mountain. The Company was badly shot up, Lang was killed, and I was wounded. I never saw the others again until after the war. The rest of us put the whole thing behind us, but Red never did, I guess. Hence his commemorative pens.

"I didn't kill him, Mrs. Hark. If I hadn't talked to Mrs. Millet about the pen, I could have stayed clear of the whole thing."

"I doubt it," Mrs. Hark said. "If the police find out that you knew him and didn't say so, it will look very suspicious indeed."

Reluctantly, Mr. Geranium accompanied the ladies to the Gambol Beach Police Station. Three hours later he was booked on suspicion of murder.

Back at her granny-pad, Mrs. Millet cried angry tears, and Mrs. Hark tried to comfort her.

* * * *

The Gambol Mini-Storage manager was not pleased with the notoriety that swept over the business. He repeatedly called Mrs. Millet to complain. In future, vacant lockers were to be secured with one of Gambol Storage's own padlocks. Why hadn't he been notified before the police were called? Did Mrs. M really try to find him? The night watchman had left Socrates in the office that night instead of out guarding the premises—the watchman was fired!—as soon as he could be replaced. Furthermore...

At last, Mrs. Millet let her answering machine take his calls. If only she had her taxes paid, he could take his job and...

But she didn't, couldn't, stop wondering about the crime. Why had the victim come to the storage yard? Why was his body placed in the locker—with those wine bottles? Did the murderer plan to use the locker, in advance? Was he outside the fence, watching and waiting for someone to leave a locker empty? That seemed unlikely.

Then who knew a locker would be empty and open? Phillip Sand, who vacated the locker, and whose answers had been so glib and ready that Sunday morning when the dead man lay inside locker E8. Anyone who knew he was vacating. Had Mr. Geranium been around on Saturday afternoon? She didn't think so.

Mrs. Millet's telephone rang. "This is Detective Clovis Jones. Chief Belgrave wants to see you—please come to the station as soon as possible."

Well, how opportune. Mrs. Millet had things to say to Chief Belgrave, too.

* * * *

At the police station, Mrs. Millet answered the Chief's questions, realizing how little she really knew about Mr.

Geranium. She had met Chief Marion Belgrave (Marion the Librarian behind his back) the year before, due to some hijacked steaks and a murdered truck driver. Even though she disliked beards and hated the reek of cigars in his office, she had learned to respect his abilities.

The Chief listened to her reasoning on the vacant locker and brushed it aside, saying, "We questioned the renter. He was out by 5:30 and didn't see anything unusual."

He opened a folder with a confidential air. "This is not for distribution, Mrs. Millet, but Joseph Rossi was charged with murder in 1950—the killing of a man who served in his outfit in Italy. He was raving mad, according to this report—not fit to stand trial. They tucked him away in a mental hospital. In 1962 he escaped and was never recaptured.

"The victim in the 1950 murder was stabbed and his body left in a shed soaked in wine, with empty bottles placed around it just like the scene in your locker, except there were three bottles instead of two. What do you make of that?"

"I don't know. What does Mr. Geranium say?"

"Says he heard about it at the time. But if Rossi was the crazy killer, how come he wound up dead? Your Mr. Geranium couldn't explain that, Mrs. Millet. His real name isn't Geranium, by the way, and he could have done the 1950 killing himself. We're checking..."

"Oh, Chief Belgrave! Surely not..." Mrs. Millet's whole being denied the thought. "When was Rossi killed? And who bought the wine—have you been able to find out?"

They were pertinent questions and the Chief answered them. "Coroner says our victim had been dead ten or twelve hours. Mr. Geranium was at home, alone, he says. And the victim bought the wine." He puffed on his half-smoked cigar. "Stop clutching at straws, Mrs. Millet. We're holding him. We haven't got a solid case yet, but there's plenty to work on."

* * * *

Mrs. Millet drove home, seething with frustration, and called Mrs. Hark. After a full report on her meeting with Chief Belgrave, she said, "I still say, who knew that locker would be empty? Phillip Sand, that's who! The Chief says that's not important. He sees the connection to Mr. Geranium and refuses to look any further! I can't stand it!"

"Maybe the Chief is right. If there was an earlier killing..."

"Can you really see Mr. Geranium pouring wine over dead bodies and setting up the empties like candlesticks? Nonsense! The other body had three wine bottles, the Chief said."

"Oh." Mrs. Hark was quick to pick up her line of thought. "Three wine bottles. In Italy, there were five soldiers. One was killed in battle. So after the first murder there were three of them left..."

"Uh-huh. And two left after Dago Red was killed; Mr. Geranium and one other—the one named Floyd Saunders. Our Phillip Sand is the right age, and the way he hung around and asked questions—like he was looking for someone. Come with me? I can get his address at the office and pick you up in twenty minutes."

* * * *

Mrs. Hark pulled on her linen jacket and hastily applied fresh makeup. She was ready and waiting when Mrs. Millet arrived in her pickup. They took the twisting road between the bean fields and turned on Highway One toward the ocean and downtown Gambol Beach.

"So Chief Belgrave thinks he's caught his killer," Mrs. Hark ventured.

"Oh, Judy, could I be that wrong?"

"Well, Mr. Geranium didn't tell us about the other man being killed or Dago Red going insane. If he's innocent, why be so secretive?"

Margaret didn't answer and looked glum as a wet cat. When they got to the traffic-choked beach area, she parked the truck on a side street near a square building with few pretensions. Mr. Sand's new apartment was on the second floor. Margaret knocked on his door, and he opened it on the chain, peering through a one-inch crack. Mrs. Hark could see boxes piled behind him and two suitcases just inside the door.

"Oh, it's you, Miz..." He recognized Margaret but didn't remember her name—or had never bothered to know it. He unchained the door and opened it.

Mrs. Hark took a good look at Mr. Sand. His name described him; sandy, thinning hair over a sandy, aging face. Medium height, sturdy arms and shoulders. He wore unpressed khaki pants, and armpit hair sprouted from a hole in his knit shirt. The only thing neat about him was his shoes; brown oxfords, highly polished. A military habit?

He answered Margaret's questions with, "I told you, and the police, too—I had all my stuff out of that locker by 5:30 and never saw anything or anybody. What more can I say?"

"I did hope you could help, Mr. Sand," Margaret persisted. "Did you hear anyone outside the fence? An innocent man may be convicted of murder if we can't find out what really happened."

"What innocent man?" Sand asked.

"Mr. Geranium. Seems he knew the dead man in the war..."

"Sorry, don't know him." He shook his head. "I can't help you ladies. As you see, I'm pretty busy..." He moved toward them, ready to close the door in their faces.

Mrs. Hark's eye fell on the front of the man's knit shirt. A pen was clipped inside his pocket—its gold top reflected a gleam of light. Without stopping to think, she plucked it out and showed it to Margaret. "Look, the pen!"

One glance and Margaret got the message. Sand saw the certainty on her face, and he got the message, too. Mrs. Hark found her arm in a steely grip. She tossed the pen toward the stairway, and screamed.

Sand slammed Mrs. Hark against the open door and pulled something from his pocket. Snick! a knife-blade popped out. He held the point to her chin. Her muscles froze in terror. Her entire life didn't pass before her; only an image of dear old Willy, dozing in his chair. Would she ever see him again?

"Pick up that pen!" Sand ordered. Stumbling, Margaret bent to comply.

"The pen. Hell, Red must have had his pen on him!" Sand sounded rational, almost apologetic, but his knife pricked Mrs. Hark's throat, and she stretched her chin a quarter inch higher.

"And your Mr. Geranium—there's only one person he could be! And now I gotta split without seeing him—what rotten luck! And what am I gonna do with you two?"

There was no doubt this man was Floyd Saunders, and he had killed Red Rossi. Mrs. Hark wanted him to admit it, but under the circumstances, it seemed unsafe to ask. Her voice wasn't working properly, either. "Wine bottles?" she bleated, and he pushed her harder against the door.

"Wine bottles! That crazy Dago and his wine bottles." He reached for Margaret, whose eyes were huge in her white face, pulled her inside and shut the door. "Why couldn't you mind your own business?"

Sand held Mrs. Hark tightly and used her body to push Mrs. Millet into the kitchen. "Sit. Put the pen on the table." He produced a roll of strong cord, and forced Mrs. Hark to tie her friend to the chair with hard, uncompromising knots.

"As for you, here you go; you ought to fit nicely." He opened a tall cupboard housing brooms and a water heater. There was just room for her body inside. "Now get in there and be quiet. You'll be able to breathe all right—see the vent holes? But don't yell, either of you! If you do, I'll have to conk you."

For a moment the sheer relief of escaping the knife flooded Mrs. Hark's body. Her knees sagged and she slumped against the water heater, uncomfortably warm to the touch. Through the cupboard door she heard Margaret wail, "But what happened? Why did you do it?"

"The little bastard jumped me, that's why! He should have known he couldn't take me. This is his knife, lady, not mine. When I came back for the last load of my stuff, there he was, drunk as a lord. He jumped me, and I damn well had to finish him off, the poor sod."

His voice sank lower and he seemed to be talking to himself—or to his dead buddies. "Sergeant de Sade, you're gloating in Hell, aren't you? Well, you won't get me. Poor old Dago Red..."

Mrs. Hark called, "Then it was self-defense! You don't have to run away. Turn yourself in and explain!"

"No thanks, honey."

Margaret said, "But Mr. Geranium may be convicted of murder! You can't let that happen..."

"Mr. Geranium can take care of himself—I'm getting out of here!"

Margaret said, "They'll find you! Stay and..."

"Not a chance. Tell you what; I'll leave the knife. I'll even leave my pen! That make you happy? All I need is an hour's head start."

Mrs. Hark heard him walk away. He came back a minute later and began pounding on the outside of the cupboard. A nail spurted through the door frame—he was boarding up the door! Her heart sank. The man thought of everything.

"Tell my buddy I've gone to find my ukulele—in case he decides to clear out, too."

Margaret echoed, "Find your ukulele?"

No answer. A few minutes later the front door slammed and all was still except for an occasional clank from the water heater. Mrs. Hark's arm hurt where Sand had grabbed it, and the balls of her feet ached in their high-heeled shoes. A broom made a tubular dent all along her left hip and thigh. Her linen jacket, crushed and soiled by God-knows-what in these tight quarters, would never be the same again.

"Margaret, are you all right?"

"No! Did you have to tie these knots so darn tight?"

"Does anybody in these apartments stay home during the day, do you think?" Mrs. Hark waited a few minutes more in case Sand came back for something and then started to yell "Help! Let us out!"

* * * *

Phillip Sand had grinned at Mrs. Millet as he nailed a board across the cupboard door, a rueful grin of apology, before he dropped the hammer and left the kitchen. Judy's yells for help weren't reaching anyone—Sand must have known there was nobody in the building, or he would have gagged them. The fact was, it was up to her, Margaret Millet, to get them out of this. She had gotten them into it.

She stretched her wrists, then made one hand as small as possible and tried to pull it out of the loop. Ouch! The coarse twine cut into her skin and refused to free her. Her hands were tied behind the chair back, so she couldn't pick at the knot with her teeth. Judy had done a good job—mustn't blame Judy; Sand made her do it, inspecting each knot for slippage as she went.

Her feet were tied to the front legs of the sturdy wooden chair, above the cross braces. Why couldn't the man have had a modern kitchen chair? The kind with legs easy to break off or nylon feet that came loose? This thing was probably solid oak under the layers of white paint, and her chances of breaking it, bound as she was, were nil.

She could move it, though. By stretching her arches, she could get enough purchase with her toes to push the chair a few inches across the floor, backward. Could she tip herself forward and walk with the chair on her back? She tried—and tried again. No go. It was just too heavy, and with her hands behind her, she couldn't get the weight off the floor.

The knife lay on the kitchen table, roughly five feet in front of her. Sand hadn't bothered to retract the blade. If she could only reach it... Slowly, inch by painful inch, Mrs. Millet wrestled the chair around and backed it toward the table.

Judy's voice was reduced to a croak by the time Mrs. Millet, prying with the hammer's claw, finally forced the cupboard door.

"You got loose!" Judy, her limbs stiffened from confinement, fell out of the cupboard.

"I made it to the knife." Mrs. Millet shook the twine cuttings off the chair, helped Judy onto it, and brought her a drink of water. She called the police, and Detective Clovis Jones arrived shortly thereafter.

When Mrs. Millet let him in, Jones lost no time in pleasantries. "The Chief thought you might try some fool thing on your own, Mrs. Millet. Well, I'm here—what happened?"

With a giddy grin, Judy said, "Well, bless ol' Marion the Li—Chief of Police! We found his murderer, that's what happened!"

About then, Jones got an eyeful of the splintered cupboard and the objects on the table. He saw the knife and he saw the gold pen, just like Mr. Geranium's. He moved closer to take a good look and gave a soft, low whistle.

* * * *

The following Saturday, Judy Hark and Mr. Geranium came to Gambol Storage, carrying paper bags. "We came to celebrate!" Judy announced. Mr. Geranium, grinning from ear to ear, pulled three plastic glasses out of his sack, lined them up in a row, and filled them with sparkling liquid from a thermos. Chilled Chianti—Italian wine.

"A toast! To Margaret Millet, Mistress of Mystery, Queen of Clues, She Who Sees the Hidden and Reveals the Unknown!"

"Amen!" Judy raised her glass.

They produced cheese rolls to go with the wine, and Mrs. Millet was so tickled she hardly knew where to look. "Oh, my goodness—you shouldn't have—let me get you a chair—what a treat! Bless you, dear friends..." She knew she was gushing, but better gush than dumbfounded silence, her usual reaction to unexpected kindness.

Business at the storage yard was slow, for once, and they celebrated with few interruptions. Judy Hark, that intrepid matchmaker, encouraged Mr. Geranium to open up and talk to them about his two nights in jail, his relief on being released, and Floyd Saunders, aka Sand, who had apparently made good his escape.

"So Floyd took Dago Red, crazy as he was," Mr. Geranium said. "Floyd always was good at hand-to-hand combat."

"Your buddy is one forceful fellow. Polite, though, I will say that," Mrs. Millet remarked.

"Polite! Is a knife to the throat polite?" Judy rubbed her neck ruefully.

"He'd never have really hurt you," Mr. Geranium said, and went on to tell them stories about his wartime buddies until Mrs. Millet felt she had known them all. Red Rossi, the volatile grandson of Italy. Martin Lang, blonde and successful with girls, killed in battle. Johnson, who lived to go back to college and become a teacher before Red killed him. And Floyd Saunders, rough and inarticulate, but a true friend. These men had been young soldiers together, a lasting bond. Now there were only two of them left, and they were old.

"I was a mere bobby-soxer then," Mrs. Millet said, remembering her own wartime youth. "The war meant sailors at the Saturday night dances and no gasoline to go to basketball games."

"In 1948, the four of us who were left had a reunion. That was when Red gave us the pens. He made a speech about it—said the pens were 'from Sergeant de Sade, a souvenir.' He'd got the idea in his poor, addled brain that the Sergeant was still alive, in Red's own body—and wanted revenge. He got crazier and crazier. In 1950 he killed Johnson, and they put him away.

"Later, by the time he escaped, my wife had died and the company I worked for had gone out of business. Dago Red out looking for me—well, it was just too much. I sold my house and car, got on a bus, and started a new life with a new name. The only person I notified was Floyd, and we lost touch with each other after a while. He must have come out here looking for me, is all I can figure. And Red must have followed him."

"I almost forgot!" Mrs. Millet cried. "Floyd said to tell you he was going to find his ukelele. Did he mean to Hawaii?"

Mr. Geranium laughed and slapped his knee. "No! He's gone to where he lost his ukelele! Good, nobody will ever find him there. Maybe I'll join him. Wait 'til I see that old son-of-a-gun. The way he set up those wine bottles—like he was crazy, too! You can't imagine what a shock it was! I expected to see Floyd's body—but it was Red."

Judy said, "Too bad he ran away. Surely, after all this time..."

"Yes, I'm sorry he took off. But he's right, you know. Standing trial for Red's killing could take years, even if he was acquitted—years we don't have any more. And what if the military started looking into what happened to Sergeant de Sade?"

Mrs. Millet munched a cheese roll and considered his words. Mr. Geranium and Floyd Saunders had given their youth to the war and spent later years hiding from a crazed killer. Why should their remaining time be sacrificed? She could never condone murder, but Floyd had killed to defend himself. Squirming on her chair, she raised her glass and said, "I hope he's never found. I wish him a happy, carefree old age!"

Judy asked, "Mr. Geranium, what is your real name?"

"My real name," Mr. Geranium said with a twinkle, "is Andrew Posey."

Andrew Posey. Mrs. Millet felt a warm surge of relief; her mystery man was no longer a mystery. Why, even her job here at Gambol Storage seemed possible—enjoyable—once again.

She took a deep breath and said, "Don't go. Stay and enjoy your new life. You'll always be Mr. Geranium to me. Why don't we go out for dinner? Would Wednesday suit you?"

♦ ♦ ♦ ♦

Margaret Searles is an ex-chemist, bookkeeper and bookstore owner who lives, writes and edits on the North Coast of California. Mrs. Millet and Mrs. Hark, her two elderly snoops, have appeared in magazines, previous SinC anthologies and four novels: *Terlingua Ale*, *Devonshire Cream*, *Filet Mignon* and *Brinyside Chowder*.

Carpe Diem

K.M. Kavanagh

Heady incense and smoldering beeswax candles scented the air and tickled Dominic's nostrils. Finding this church had saved him.

Latin prayers flowed from his mouth with practiced ease, faltering only when he uttered, "*Libera nos a malo.*" Dominic was a strong believer in deliverance from evil, but the phrase tied him to his haunted past. With his back to the worshippers, he smoothed his beard and nodded to the nervous altar boy. He raised the chalice to the crucifix and as the bell rang three times, drank the sacred wine.

Such power! But the strong rush of fermented grapes wasn't what overloaded his senses. It was the faithful crowd—both high society and the downtrodden in their respective places—who had gathered for Mass. Rapt attention was a new experience. His audience listened as never before, hanging on every word he uttered. Dominic moved forward, and several pairs of eyes tracked his progress.

The wool layer scratched at his leggings, but he loved the swooshing sound made by the large linen robe as he approached the wooden communion rail. "*Corpus Domini nostri Jesu Christi…*"started the litany for each kneeling supplicant to receive the blessed host. Then he spotted someone whom he'd expected; she was *early*. He moved methodically down the line, brushing aside the excitement that grew inside him.

* * * *

When blood debts are paid, honor and family are restored.

Jorge had drummed the credo into him, but Dominic didn't fully comprehend its meaning. Though usually instructive, his mentor had insisted he would only understand once his mission was completed. Jorge, a man who masked his face, always worked from a hidden agenda. With resolve, Dominic shut out these disturbing thoughts. If he didn't move soon, he might lose his chance. *Carpe diem!* Another of Jorge's teachings, and one Dominic understood and believed.

He'd watched the penitent enter the confessional from a shadowy corner. She wore a veil that failed to obscure her mature features. His heart beat faster knowing the woman was *her.* Dominic blew his breath out slowly, noting how the sacramental wine lingered on his tongue. He savored this a moment, then made his decision. He entered the priest's side of the confessional and parted the thick velvet curtain. As he leaned toward the perforated wooden partition, a voice roughened by age whispered, "Bless me, Padre, for I have sinned."

It didn't take long for the woman to recount her sins. Perhaps, in the latter stage of life, desires of the flesh had been burned from memory, past transgressions long forgotten. If need be, Dominic would *force* a confession.

"Good lady, I hear hesitation. Have you overlooked a sin or two?"

The woman gasped, then covered it with a phlegmy cough.

Not surprising. He'd delivered the question with the bluntness of a Spanish Inquisitor. He'd seen them in action. Questions rapidly hurled at the accused, but answers never mattered. *It was fixed.* Once the Inquisitors had a victim in their grasp, death soon followed. Briefly, Dominic envisioned the woman burning at a stake. Though many had been targeted for that fate, she had bribed the right officials to stay *that* execution.

"No other misdeeds, Padre."

He smiled. Despite her reluctance, he knew a confession was imminent. "If you suddenly met our Heavenly Father, wouldn't you want your soul cleansed of sin?"

The woman began to cry softly.

"Repent now. God will forgive you."

"I once stole something…" she began in a shaky voice.

Dominic heard the passion. He knew she was frightened. "God forgives thieves—"

"—I stole something *valuable*."

She began crying again, but Dominic was relentless. The woman must repent. "The end is near; confess *all* your sins."

No answer. Only the sounds of a woman sobbing her heart out. He felt nothing.

"Our Lord Jesus died on the cross for our sins," he whispered. *That* always opened the flood gates.

One last sob, then she said, "I stole a life."

Dominic had never heard the story from these lips. He imagined Blanca once again as a young chambermaid, lusting after the rich Spanish landowner, Juan Castillo. The man possessed many secrets; this woman only one of them.

"I took the pearls. Pearls that he promised to me! When his wife Carmen found me in the bedchamber, pearls clutched in my hands, she screamed, '*Blanca, las perlas son míos. Juan es mío.*'"

"I argued that the pearls and Juan were *mine*. Why should Carmen stake a claim after so many years of indifference? Jealousy! When she yanked the ivory combs—Juan's gift—from my hair, anger consumed me. I crushed her skull with a silver candlestick."

Juan was then solely hers. But not for long, she explained. A month later, Blanca caught Juan with a scullery maid. Soon after, her love died with him. She took his life, gold and jewels, then fled from Spain. Blanca's loud sobs punctuated the end of her story. Dominic's hands trembled, an unusual response. Because he'd waited so long? His mentor was right. *Carpe diem!*

Heart beating loud and fast, Dominic seized the day. He slipped into Blanca's side of the confessional before her two guards could reach them from the back of the church. He ripped off the veil, brushed aside the hennaed curls and stared into a tear-blotched face that had been burned into his memory by hatred. More lined now, but easily recognizable by the tiny mole beside her bee stung lips. Juan Castillo had loved that mouth, but the way it formed a surprised "O" fueled Dominic's rage. He ripped the pearls from her throat and wrapped strong hands around her neck.

"God forgives you, Blanca de la Ortiz, but *I* do not."

His hawk-like Castillo nose must've given him away. Dark eyes that had rounded in fear transformed into narrow slits inflamed with hate.

"The tribunal accepted my *donations.* I've paid, you bastard!"

"No, *Juan* paid with his life; *I've* paid ever since!"

"You don't understand…"

"It's too late, hag," he whispered gruffly.

The old witch spat at him, then clawed his face. He tightened his grip on her neck. With a slow, steady pressure he squeezed life's breath from her. She kicked her feet frantically, trying desperately to dislodge his strong grip. Above clanking armor, he heard yelling and the pounding of booted feet headed in their direction. The end *was* near. Instead of strangling Blanca slowly as he'd planned, he twisted her neck in one fluid motion. He felt the vertebrae separate violently. The eerie cracking sound satisfied his rage.

He shoved the lifeless body aside and whispered, "At last, my blood debt is paid."

Dominic pulled a rose from the tunic hidden beneath his robe and dropped it on the corpse. He dove through the velvet curtains, tripped a guard and grabbed his sword roughly from him. He parried the other guard's lunge and knocked him into the fellow sprawled on the floor. They tangled, heavy armor weighing them down. Still garbed in a holy man's clothing, Dominic sprinted from the church. Clouds of dust rose on the dirt path as he streaked toward the bazaar.

He followed the route he had staked out earlier. Not one villager watched his rapid retreat; the crowd was captivated by a jester juggling oranges. Dominic quickly stripped off the robe and tossed it behind a bush. Only the woolen tunic and the leggings of his cover trade now remained. No longer a priest, once again a travelling actor. Moving quickly past piles of fragrant horse dung, he tore the beard from his face, surprised at how it stung. He dropped the facial hair into a boiling cauldron on an open campfire and made a beeline for the caravan.

The horses seemed as eager to leave as he, stamping their feet and snorting. The colorful pageant and troupe wagons had already regrouped beyond the town's tall wooden gates. Dominic would blend in with other actors and disappear.

If only his sins would vanish as easily, he thought. Jorge, his mentor, had always told him the kills were sanctioned. If that were true, Dominic would probably roast in hell for knocking the priest senseless and stealing his robe. But would Dominic pay for executing a killer? Not according to Jorge.

And what about the other deaths commissioned by *Sub Rosa?* So many layers of secrets. The church had condemned many for witchcraft and other sins that Dominic now began to question. Those who publicly cried out against these dealings were quietly taken out. He believed that Queen Isabella and King Ferdinand had executed many rich aristocrats for treason and other serious crimes against the crown, while lining the royal coffers. Dominic had lost count of the victims he'd targeted while posing as a travelling actor. Jorge had argued long and often that such assassinations served both God and country. Therefore, these deaths would not mar their souls.

"We will never be free," Dominic whispered to a horse that neighed as he strode by. He marched toward the last wagon in the long caravan. He kicked a rock and shrugged off the uneasiness that had invaded his thoughts lately. Too much reflection would destroy his skill. He smiled. No matter the personal cost, he had succeeded. His debt to his brother Juan was finally paid.

It had taken years to hunt down the once hauntingly beautiful chambermaid, Blanca. Curious about the ways of men and women, young Dominic had hidden in Juan's bedchamber behind a screen. The hard knife of lovemaking that Juan had described to the boy was unlike the one that she'd plunged into his chest. The cruel face that hovered over his older brother as she killed him was etched forever in his memory. Blanca's face had filled his nightmares and fueled the hate.

An absentee father, his mother and brother dead, and another sibling missing: Blanca cruelly eliminated Dominic's last chance at familial ties. He grew up and traveled through the provinces and townships of Europe as a member of an acting troupe. While performing, he always searched the crowd for the face of the woman who'd murdered his beloved elder brother. Mentally, he often replaced his victims' faces with hers, thereby obliterating his pain with their destruction.

Juan's death had started the cycle of killing and revenge—a talent which served Dominic well as a *Sub Rosa* assassin. With practice, he'd learned to dispatch his targets with cold precision. Though assigned, this time the kill had been personal and satisfying. His brother Juan would've been as proud as a father.

Dominic took one last glance around before climbing into the Master of Secrets' personal wagon. Jorge would not mind; he seemed to be elsewhere as usual. Morality plays required people with behind-the-sets talent. Machinery which produced the special effects—flying angels, hellfire, trap doors—needed precision and planning. These were things Jorge produced easily, while remaining in the shadows. A man who controlled much power, his mentor truly was the Master of All Secrets, Dominic thought with a smirk.

Always, Jorge wore a cloth mask that hid features below his flashing dark eyes. The effect was quite formidable. When he barked a command, all obeyed without question. Especially Alfonso, Jorge's bright, but sniveling assistant. The young assassin learned early on that was only an act. He knew Alfonso's connection to the crown. He owed his life and freedom to both Isabella *and Jorge*. Someday, Alfonso would be forced to show gratitude for his huge debt. Dominic smiled. He shared a much different relationship with his mentor. One moored in friendship, yet somehow almost as close as family. Perhaps their secret lives bound them together?

With loud shouts and whip cracks, the lead wagons began their journey. They headed away from the direction that Dominic longed to explore. He sighed. He often dreamed of meeting Jorge at the docks, where they could book passage on a ship sailing to the West Indies. Some claimed the world ended there; other explorers, like Columbus, believed differently. In either case, those sailing men truly knew freedom. Dominic sighed. This was a dream friends shared while drinking ale.

Jorge's driver yelled, a whip cracked, and the wagon lurched forward. The curtains parted, light filtered in and a tall man's silhouette filled the opening. He stood confidently, easily blocking the assassin's escape. As Dominic readied himself for a fight, the smell of oranges wafted toward him, and he relaxed. "Jorge! I didn't know you juggled."

"There's much you don't know about me." Jorge turned his back on Dominic while working the knot on the string of his mask.

Dominic was surprised. His mentor had left his neck vulnerable. Did Jorge trust him that much?

"What's left to learn?"

"With the theatre troupe I travelled everywhere as the Master of Secrets, but—"

"—that was a cover for the real secret as my mentor?"

"Yes, but before you joined, I started out training horses. Set machinery requires special handling, but animals need even more attention."

"Which occupation was more difficult?"

"Assassin."

Made sense. You needed to fully understand the tricks of the trade in order to teach them. Dominic studied Jorge's back as his mentor yanked the knot free. For some reason, he thought again of Blanca's declaration before her death. "Was Blanca sanctioned?"

"Not through official channels. *I* set that in motion. It was only fair that you performed the deed."

"Yes, but why?"

"As your mentor, I could not be free until you learned all that I could teach. Now that you have reached our goal, your work is done."

Jorge turned abruptly, and faced him sans mask. Surprisingly, a handsome man, not the horror that gossips had speculated upon. Dark eyes glittering, he smiled, advancing slowly toward Dominic. The young man tensed. Despite their age difference, his mentor had skills that far surpassed his. He hoped the end would be swift and painless.

To Dominic's surprise, Jorge hugged him tightly, then kissed both cheeks. "By destroying Juan's killer, you have revenged and honored our father. You've earned your freedom, *my* brother."

Shocked beyond words, Dominic stared at the Castillo hawk like nose, silent as everything slid into place. Now he understood.

"What would you like to do now?" Jorge asked.

"See how good you are with horses." Dominic smiled.

For once, Jorge was speechless.

"*Carpe diem,* brother," said Dominic with a wink.

Dominic dove through the curtain with Jorge close behind. The young assassin tossed the driver from the wagon as his brother commanded the reins. Jorge swung the wagon in an opposite direction from the caravan.

"But who will work the sets?" Dominic yelled to his brother over the pounding hooves of the horses.

"Alfonso. He paid handsomely for his new life and was glad to settle his debt."

"Where are we headed, Jorge?"

"Where men can truly be free!"

Dominic closed his eyes blissfully. He imagined the smell of the sea and wind whipping through his hair, could almost taste the salt spray upon his face. He opened his eyes and glanced at his brother, who seemed focused, but relaxed. When Jorge turned, the brothers smiled in unison, similar features lit brightly and gladdened by full hearts. Working together, they'd seized the day.

♦ ♦ ♦ ♦

Author's Note

Christopher Columbus, Queen Isabella and King Ferdinand are well-known historical figures whose efforts greatly influenced their world in the 15th century and beyond that time.

In days of old, assassinations were contracted by secret tribunals, highly placed officials connected to church and/or crown, and men with great wealth and influence desiring more. These assassinations were usually directed at members of the royal lineage and other wealthy individuals who possessed power.

Historically, there's no proof that King Ferdinand or Queen Isabella had anything to do with the queen's brother, Alfonso, being poisoned. In real life, poor Alfonso never recovered. In *Carpe Diem*, the royal sibling survived the attempt on his life, so that his actions could affect the outcome of this story.

K.M. Kavanagh's award-winning stories are featured in *Dogwood Tales, Gone Coastal* and *Never Safe*. You'll find *Gone Coastal* characters in *Rock of Morro Bay*. Her novel, *Wing It 1,* will be published soon. A lover of classic cars, she dreams of moving beloved husband and their '49 Woodie to Cambria, CA.

The SomeWhen Murder

Susan Tuttle

Southern California's Grapevine is no place to be driving when the weather doesn't cooperate. Rain had begun icing the pavement by 8:00 am. An hour later wind and snow were howling for blood. My shortcut home began to look more like a long walk off a short pier. I should have known better. My karma sucks.

I'd gotten as far as Gorman when they closed the road. Pansy asses, I thought, though to tell the truth, I'd grown weary of slip-sliding up that steep grade. My hands and wrists ached from wrestling with the Prius' wheel, and a rip-snorter of a headache bided its time beneath my skull. My eyes were doing their wonky thing again, throwing up double images, here and there, quick visions of the past brought to me courtesy of my so-called psychic "gifts." Stopping for the night seemed like a damned good idea.

Until I stopped.

Gorman isn't famous for luxury accommodations. Truckers already possessed all the rooms of the one seedy motel by the time I arrived. I had, I was told, two choices. I could blanket-bunk on the lobby floor with the other stranded unfortunates—including wailing babies, sugar-hyped kids and anxious pets, not all of them four-legged—or I could brave wind and snow to see if the MacLarrens, who sometimes let rooms for exorbitant prices, still had one left.

I looked at the snake some toad-brained adolescent had turned loose on the lobby floor and decided to take my chances with the weather. I struggled against the wind for three endless blocks, stopping halfway to catch my breath by hanging onto a memorial sign for a young woman named Amelia Sanchez who'd vanished over a hundred years ago. I was half-frozen and sopping wet when I arrived at the MacLarren's.

Still, it was a smart decision. The place was warm, dry and clean, even if it hadn't been updated in seventy or so years. And there were two rooms vacant. The smaller one in front, on the second floor, overlooked the main drag, not that I could see anything but sideways-driven snow. It had a window seat, a rocking chair, and wallpaper with Victorian cabbage roses that had faded to a dull brown. It reminded me of my grandmother's San Francisco house, so I let nostalgia make the room choice for me.

It raised a few brows when I signed the register: Skylark, Private Investigator, Los Osos, Ca; though I'm not sure which surprised them most, the single name or my occupation. I had to show my driver's license to prove my one name status before they'd hand me the room key. By then it was late and my mind was shutting off. I sipped down a complimentary hot chocolate, climbed into the surprisingly comfortable brass double bed, burrowed under a worn handmade quilt and within minutes fell asleep.

A scream yanked me from a misty dream around 3:00 am, a short high burst of panic followed by a longer wail of pure terror. I leapt from the bed, my heart hammering in my chest, not entirely sure where I was. Then I recognized the window seat and rocking chair in the dim light filtering through the heavy drapes. Ah. Gorman. MacLarren's. I was still wrapping my mind around that when two shots echoed in the street outside.

I dove for my pistol on the nightstand, then crouched motionless, listening. Nothing. I sidled to the window and parted the drapes. The wind had died down. The snow had almost stopped. Fitful moonlight glimmered on the few flakes still drifting in the air. Nothing else moved.

But I had heard that scream. And the shots. If someone was out there, injured, he or she could bleed to death by morning. Or freeze. I stifled a sigh, pulled on my clothes, went into the hall and listened. No stirring anywhere. It seemed the MacLarrens and their other guests had not heard the noises. Strange, I thought as I let myself out of the house.

Dark stillness greeted me. No street lamps, no lights in any nearby houses, no movement on the street. The wind had driven snow up onto the porch. The pristine sheet stretched across the deck, down the steps, over the yard to the street, then across the road to the field beyond where it vanished into the night. Not a footstep marred the smooth surface. Except—I stepped cautiously down the stairs and along the front walk—there, out near the street. A dark patch.

I inched closer, eyes and ears alert, then hunkered down beside the spot, uncomfortably aware that nylon and Velcro running shoes afforded little protection for sockless feet. I reached out and touched the inky splotch. My fingers came away red. I sniffed: rusty iron. Blood.

My heart again thudded against my ribs. Blood? I rose and firmed my grip on the gun. How can that be? I looked again at the smooth white sheet of snow surrounding me, my footprints the only disturbance marks in sight.

And the wind kicked up. A frigid gust threw a flurry of flakes in my face, blinding me. A roar filled my ears. I turned away but the snow cloud followed me, seemed to attack my eyes, my mouth. I had trouble breathing. I staggered a bit, hands raised for protection. And the night exploded with noise and motion.

"Hee-yah!" someone yelled. Muffled thuds echoed in the air; metal jangled, leather creaked. Something raced past me, just inches away. Its violent wake spun me around.

"What the hell?" I said, trying to blink the snow from my eyes.

"Hey! Watch out!" a deep voice shouted.

Then something rammed into me. I felt hands scrabble for a hold as my feet left the ground. Then somehow I was down, half-buried in snow, a body atop me. My head hit something hard and everything vanished in a blast of blinding light.

* * * *

Awareness returned with a shock. A pile driver had taken up residence in my head, working with such energy that my stomach heaved. My left shoulder burned and my ass felt numb. My left elbow and wrist throbbed. I lay on a soft surface; heavy covers did their vain best to counteract my half-frozen backside. It took a moment for memory to return, but amid the gunshots and snowflakes, noise and confusion, I found no hint of how I'd gotten inside.

I squinted against brightness as much as pain when I finally pried my lids apart and looked around. How long was I out? I wondered, blinking at the sunglare streaming through the uncurtained window. Who brought me into the house? And what happened to the drapes? Something was majorly wrong here, but the dueling cannon in my head wouldn't allow me enough clear thought to work it out.

I struggled up, fighting nausea all the way to a sitting position. I held onto the edge of the mattress to keep from tumbling to the floor while I waited for a semblance of equilibrium to return—and my stomach to regain its rightful position south of my throat—then gave the room another glance.

And my eyes once again saw what wasn't there, echoes of the past.

It was the same room I'd checked into a few hours earlier, and yet it wasn't. Clothing hung on pegs where the old oak dresser should be. A dry sink complete with china ewer and basin replaced the lady's desk where I'd parked my laptop. The wall sconces held candles, not bulbs, and the cabbage roses on the walls shimmered a brilliant maroon. Curtains did cover the window, but the filmy lace did little to cut the glare of sun on snow.

Damn this paranormal crap, I thought, blinking to bring the present back into focus. A soft tap sounded at the door and broke my concentration.

"Come in," I said.

A man entered and stood in the shadows just inside the doorway.

"How are you doing?" he asked in a deep voice that rasped like a file on hardwood.

"I've been better." I turned my head to look at him and the sledge hammer in my temples blindsided me. I shut my eyes and hunched my shoulders. "What—"

"I regret that you were injured. But if I hadn't grabbed you, you'd have been run over. I doubt Old Ben could see you in the storm."

"Run over?" I twisted my upper body toward him very slowly and cracked my lids apart. "I wasn't even in the street."

"Then why did you need rescuing?" A smile danced around the corners of his sharply-chiseled mouth. "And you're welcome, by the way."

I dismissed him with a wave, pretty sure this had to be a psychic dream. Or nightmare. Maybe if I moved I'd wake up. But when I gathered myself to stand I realized I wore not jeans and ski parka but a long-sleeved, high-necked linen blouse and an ankle-length skirt of dark blue wool. My gasp sounded loud even to me.

"Your clothing is drying by the kitchen fire," the man said, "along with your, ah, footwear. My sister-in-law's friend, Marisol, made you comfortable. She was not happy I brought you here, given the events of the past week, but I could not very well leave you unconscious in the snow. Especially since no one knew who you were."

He took a step forward into the light. He was so tall his

head almost brushed the ceiling, and handsome in an angular way. Olive complexioned. Straight black hair and tomahawk cheekbones spoke of Native ancestry in the not-too-distant past. I wondered which pro team he dribbled for.

"Who are you?" I asked.

"Phillip Faurot. Your," he paused a moment and I caught a flash of confusion in his eyes, "outer garment was torn. Marisol is attempting to mend it."

Rip-stop nylon isn't mendable, I thought. She should know that. Then his earlier words penetrated the lessening pain in my head.

"The past week? What events?" I asked. His eyes went flat.

"My niece has vanished. And her husband was shot to death two days ago."

Memories bombarded me. The screams. The gunshots. I slid to my feet, grabbed the brass footboard until the room stopped rocking, and looked at the bedside table.

"Where's my Glock?" He frowned a question at me and I shook my head. "My weapon."

"Oh. Glock. That's what this is called?" He pulled my pistol from his belt and handed it to me. "I've never seen anything like it. There's no cylinder for bullets." He caressed the six-shooter holstered to his right leg and I could tell he'd played with the Glock, tried to fire it. Lucky for him I'd not chambered a round before he took me down in the snow. "And I found this in your outer garment." He took my cell phone from his coat pocket and gave it to me. "What does 'No Service' mean?"

I stared at him. Thoughts shifted in my head, moving into a place I didn't want to go, making pictures I didn't want to see. I looked around the room again, noting the candles and kerosene, the ewer and basin, the long skirts and high-necked blouses on the pegs. And Faurot not knowing what a Glock or a cell phone was, calling a ski parka an 'outer garment.' I shook my head in denial, but I couldn't keep my big mouth from opening and plunging me further into the nightmare.

"We're in Gorman, right?" I asked and he nodded. "What's the date?"

"December fourteenth."

"And the year?"

He looked at me as though I'd lost my mind, but he answered.

"Eighteen eighty-six."

* * * *

"I'd like to see it," I said.

Philip Faurot had already introduced me to the household. His sister-in-law, Florence, had disheveled brown hair, watery hazel eyes and drooping shoulders. She looked diminished by her husband's death a year earlier, crushed by current events and fearful of everything. She waved away my sympathy with a flutter of her sodden hankie, then burst into tears. Her friends, Jose and Marisol Garcia, had moved in after Florence's husband died to help her convert the huge home into a boarding house. Neither appreciated my presence if their frowning displeasure was any indication. I had the feeling Jose, a teller at the bank, would be taken to task behind closed doors just for rising when I entered the room.

The bank manager, George Rankin, who looked like Santa Claus in mufti, also rented a room from Florence. Sheriff Brady Pierce rounded out the group in the family parlor, having dropped in to check on "the little lady." I assumed that meant me, though at five-nine I wasn't a "little" anything. Pierce had a jolly avuncular look until you noticed the calculating beady eyes that lapped up details like a cat with a bowl of cream.

"The body, Philip?" I said when no one moved. "Maybe I can help."

"Wal, now, lil' lady," the sheriff said, hitching up his drooping pants just like in a B-grade Western, "no point in upsettin' yore delicate sensibilities with this."

"Don't be ridiculous," I said, and Pierce's eyes narrowed. "My sensibilities haven't been delicate since I was five years old."

I looked at Philip, who nodded at a door in the back wall. When I moved toward it, the sheriff blocked my way. He kept a neutral smile on his weathered face, but his eyes darkened with hostility. His low growl slid around me like hot cooking oil.

"This ain't none 'a yore binness, ma'am."

"Sheriff, it's all right," Philip said. "She has some experience in this."

Philip had scoffed at first when I'd speculated that somehow I'd been thrown back in time. But the presence of both Glock and cell phone, to say nothing of the Velcro-adorned shoes roasting by the fire, had argued in my favor and he'd finally admitted a half-amused belief. Still, there was a thread of steel in his voice that brooked no opposition when he confronted Brady Pierce on my behalf. The sheriff glared at him and took a grudging step aside so I could enter the unheated back porch. All four men crowded in behind me.

The body lay on its back on planks balanced atop two stools. Miguel Sanchez had been handsome. Not much over twenty-five, I estimated. He was thin and wiry, with appealing dark stubble on his sculptured cheeks, dried mud clinging to his boots and a bloom of rusty red on his chest. I leaned close to the wound, the sheriff near enough to memorize my every movement, and sniffed. An odor of cordite clung to the area. Tiny black dots stippled the washed-out blue fabric of his shirt.

"He either knew the shooter, or trusted him," I said. Then I lifted my eyes and found myself staring into the gamin face of a young boy on the other side of the table. I straightened up with a gasp.

"Joseph! Son, you should not be in here," Philip said. "Leave, please. Now."

The little pipsqueak, who looked about twelve, muttered something that earned a scowl from Philip, but the sheriff's words stopped another remonstration. And Joseph stayed rooted to the spot.

"How can you say he knew—" The sheriff shook his head. "You can't know that."

"Yes, I can. The shot was from no more than three feet away." I pointed and they all bent over the body. "See the speckles on his shirt? Those are powder burns and they mean a close shot. Where was he found? And when?"

"Around three in the morning. The shots woke us," Philip said. "He was in the middle of the street. Where you were standing."

I shook my head. That was wrong. In my timeframe the blood was on the sidewalk, not in the street. Then I realized the road must have migrated a few feet over the hundred plus years of its existence, a common occurrence before civic surveyors and property taxes multiplied across the nation.

I scanned the body again, noting bright pink flecks of what looked like stone and a few wood shavings caught in the mud on his boots, scratches on his cheek and left hand, and the lack of a holster at his hip. Strange that he would leave the house in the dead of night without his gun, especially in the still-wild West of the late 1800s.

"Did you remove his gun belt?" I asked.

"He wasn't wearing one," the sheriff said.

"More proof he was probably lured out by someone he knew," I murmured. "But why? And how does it connect with Amelia's disappearance?"

I took a steadying breath and laid my hand on Miguel's shoulder, then closed my eyes for a moment. The lines were there when I opened my lids, delicate traceries of light that connected Miguel to those with whom he'd had significant dealings in the weeks before his death. I still felt faint vestiges of the terror I'd experienced the first time this had happened to me. I don't know how I'd have kept my sanity had I not had a mentor to help me understand and harness this part of my psychic curse. Unfortunately, hard as I tried, I still couldn't make it stop.

I don't know what my face showed, but little Joseph's dark brown eyes widened and I could feel his gaze locked on me as I turned to survey the others in the room. A barely-discernible line wobbled in Philip's direction and my heart gave a tiny thud of relief. The finer the line, the less involved the contact, according to my mentor, Bass Erhler. A stronger light looped toward the bank manager. Two thick ropes connected to both the sheriff and Jose Garcia. And, most strange of all, one bright, glowing line arrowed straight through the doorway into the inner parlor. To Miguel's mother-in-law? I walked over, leaned against the doorjamb and watched the light, attached not to Florence, but to family "friend" Marisol, slowly fade away.

Interesting.

I thought about the light lines after dinner as I walked around the little enclave of houses in a borrowed coat and shawl, the place too small in my estimation to rate the title of hamlet, much less town. Philip and Joseph I could dismiss. Philip said they'd arrived only three weeks ago, and the faintness of his connection proved he had only a passing association with Miguel. The bank manager would have strong ties to many townsfolk, since there was only the one bank, so his thicker line made sense. That probably wasn't worth worrying about. But the sheriff, Jose Garcia and his wife, Marisol; something was going on there. Those were very strong light ropes. I'd need to keep an eye on those three.

I put on my "make nice" smile and listened to what gossip I could, though most residents shut their mouths when they spotted the stranger in their midst. Still, I had a good idea of Gorman's layout and the townsfolk's relationships by the time I trudged up Florence's front steps and let myself into the darkened house. A small kerosene lamp had been left near the door, the wick trimmed low. I stood a moment, warming my hands in the meager heat, listening for movement upstairs, but all was still. So I lifted the lamp and headed for the back porch. I wanted another look at Miguel Sanchez's boots.

The pink flecks were stone, and jagged as though chipped carelessly from a larger deposit. The color reminded me of my friend Rhoda's necklace, lovely polished tourmaline teardrops set in sterling silver filigree. She'd inherited it from a great aunt, along with an odd little story of how the stones had been found. Something about a stream, or was it a cave? Or was it something I'd read about?

A board creaked, and the thought vanished as I spun toward the door. Philip's son stood there in nightdress and cap, a miniature version of his father. His big brown eyes glittered in the lamplight like bright stars in his face.

"Joseph, isn't it?" I asked. He nodded. "Why are you up? Are you spying on me?"

"Are you a *bruja?*" he asked, startling me.

"A witch? Why would you think that?"

"What you said: That Miguel knew, that the killer stood close to him. Only a *bruja* could know what happened in the past."

I tried my best not to laugh.

"It's science, Joseph, not witchcraft. Unburnt powder grains will land near the wound if the shooter is close enough. All I did was look for them."

He stared at me, his face solemn, then held out his hand.

"I found this," he said.

On his palm lay a large, sparkling black jet button. The two-inch-long teardrop was an inch wide at one end and tapered to a sharp point at the other.

"It fell out of Miguel's hand when they picked him up," Joseph whispered. "No one noticed. I didn't," he looked at the doorway and shivered, "know who to give it to."

I wondered just how much this young boy, invisible to the adults around him, had seen and heard. I wanted to question him, but he was already scared enough. He didn't need a furtive midnight conversation with a strange woman in a room housing a dead body adding to his nightmares. It could wait until tomorrow.

I took the button, warmed by his body heat, and slid it into my pocket.

"Thank you, Joseph. This is a good clue. You're a smart kid. Too smart to believe that science is witchcraft, right?"

Joseph gave me a grin, then spun around and raced from the room. I followed more slowly, wondering if the button in my pocket had caused the scratches on Miguel's cheek and hand. The point was certainly sharp enough. Perhaps if I could find its owner, and the source of the wood shavings and tourmaline chips on Miguel's boots, I could solve the murder, find Amelia, and be transported back to my own time before they gave me up for lost and auctioned off my possessions. A twenty-first century forensics lab wouldn't hurt, either.

I headed for the bank after lunch the next day. I'd spent the morning questioning Florence and Marisol. Both said they had been asleep when Miguel died, and were roused by the sound of the shots. Then I asked about the day Amelia vanished. Florence held tight to Marisol's hand and wept out her guilt. She usually made the deposits, but she'd had a sick headache that day and had sent Amelia to the bank in her place. Marisol claimed to be in the kitchen, working on the evening meal, unaware until dinnertime that Amelia was gone. But her fingers played with frayed threads on the upholstery and her eyes held a note of disdain. Her answers sounded mechanical and rehearsed. It made me wonder what she was hiding.

I heard what I expected from Jose Garcia at the bank: Asleep when Miguel was shot, in his teller cage when Amelia left the bank. The other tellers confirmed his story. George Rankin remembered seeing Amelia in the bank, though the manager claimed not to have spoken to her. He seemed a bit reticent with me at first, shy despite his white-bearded, jolly Saint Nicholas appearance. But when I asked about all the building I'd seen on my walk, he became more expansive.

"We're growing bigger and better," he said. "New people settle here every week, though some have recently moved away. We've had to add two new rooms onto the school building. The city fathers have big plans for Gorman."

He gave me a wink worthy of Kris Kringle himself. I smiled at him, wondering what he'd think of the twenty-first century pit stop Gorman had become.

"It must be hard to transport building materials up here. Is there a lumber mill in the area?" I asked, thinking of the shavings on Miguel's boots.

"Oh, no, not for years now. The stream's too far away, and doesn't generate enough power anyway. We bring pre-cut boards in. Expensive, but Gorman is worth it."

That's what you think, I said to myself, then thanked him and left, wondering if it was too far to walk to that old abandoned mill. It was a good bet that Miguel Sanchez had been out there close to his death. Looking for Amelia? Had he seen something that led to the shooting?

My mind sorted possibilities as I wandered the streets, not really paying attention to where I was headed. I just needed to think. Suddenly, someone grabbed my arm, pulled me into a narrow alley between the buildings and shoved me against the rough-hewn siding. Sheriff Pierce leaned close, his body pressed against mine, and hissed into my ear.

"You bin sticking that nose 'a yores where it don't belong, lil' lady. Be a whole lot safer fer ya if'n ya were somewheres else. You git my meanin'?"

I pushed him away and he allowed it. The moment I felt his solid bulk beneath my hands I knew I hadn't the strength to make him do anything he wasn't prepared to do.

"Why, Sheriff," I cooed, holding a tight rein on my anger—who was he to manhandle me like this?—"I didn't know you cared."

"I got 'nough to deal with," he growled, shaking a thick finger in my face, "I don't need no meddling female causing trouble. Ya ain't welcome 'round here. There's a stage leavin' in the mornin'. Be on it."

He turned and strode away without a backward glance. I had to laugh. Talk about a B-grade Western; I'd just been told to get out of Dodge. If only I had control over that, I thought as I made my way back to the house, wondering which side the sheriff was on.

I arrived just as the others were leaving. Philip was treating them all to dinner at the stage depot cafe. He asked me to join them but I declined, citing exhaustion as an excuse. Marisol's coat sported buttons that matched the one Joseph had found, and though none were missing, the second from the top didn't quite match the others. I wanted some uninterrupted time to search her room.

I waved them off and headed upstairs to the Garcia's back bedroom. It was locked, but the skeleton key from my room got me in just fine. The large room, twice the size of mine, held a roll-top desk, a small settee before the fireplace, and a huge wardrobe along with a lovely mahogany sleigh bed. Still, the search didn't take long; within ten minutes I found a sheaf of papers hidden in a hatbox at the back of the wardrobe. There were letters threatening local landowners if they didn't leave town, original deeds in those landowners' names, and a series of deeds for the same properties with Marisol's name on them. Many had smears, as though blotched by water drops, accounting for the duplications. An amateur, working his or her way to a professional-looking product? I wondered. Or a terrified woman whose daughter was being held hostage, forced to do as she was bid? At the very bottom I found an assay report. Beneath the land covered, I assumed, by the forged deeds, lay a possibly-rich vein of gold.

"It always comes down to money," I murmured.

"*Si*. A lot of it, *puta*."

I jumped at the sound of her voice and cursed myself for carelessness. I hadn't heard her mount the stairs or open the door. The gun looked like a toy in her hand, but I knew that at a distance of less than five feet the derringer was as deadly as any full-size weapon. I dropped the documents, raised my hands slowly, fingers spread, and edged backward toward the small table beside the settee.

"So it was you, Marisol," I said. "You and Jose. How did you know the gold was there?" She smirked at me and I decided to take her down a peg or two. "The tourmaline, right? It's often found with gold deposits, especially in California. You found the pretty pink stone and when you dug for more you struck gold."

"How do you know that?" She jerked the little gun from side to side and I stopped moving.

"I read a lot." I gave her my smirk. "And Miguel had chips of tourmaline in the mud on his boots."

"I knew you were *trabajo, puta*, coming from nowhere with all your nosy questions," Marisol said. "Why didn't you stay out of it?"

"It's not my nature. I assume you also kidnapped Amelia, and are using her to force her mother to forge the deeds you need. Why? Can't you and Jose read and write?"

"*Silencio!*"

But I didn't want to be quiet. I wanted to distract her until I could figure out how to get away, or take her down. I wasn't about to be shot, killed and buried a hundred years before I was even born.

"And Amelia's where? At the old sawmill?" Marisol's eyes flickered and I smiled. "Miguel had sawdust on his boots, too. He found out about the deeds and where Amelia was," I added, wondering why he'd not rescued her if he'd been at the mill, "and that's why you killed him."

"What makes you think I kill him, *puta*?"

"Because, bitch," I said, returning the insult in English and moving closer to the table, "Miguel pulled a button off your coat when he fell. The replacement doesn't quite match. Did you really think no one would notice?"

Her eyes glittered as she fingered the button in question. Then she laughed. The malice in the sound sent shivers down my back.

"You know nothing. *Nada.*" She took a step closer to me, and I put the little side table between us. "I was there, yes, but I did not kill him. I was too busy kissing him."

I let my hands drop as the implication washed over me.

"Jose killed Miguel?" I shook my head. "Why would you have an affair, betray your husband, with all this at stake?" I gestured at the documents scattered on the bed. "That doesn't make sense."

"Jose. Pah!" She spat. "*Que cretino*. I told Miguel to get rid of him weeks ago, before he learned of our scheme. But Miguel, he had no *cojone*s, and now my lover is dead and my *mi hermano* thinks he is in charge."

"Jose is your brother? Gad!"

"We fool you all," she said. "*Gringos estupidos.*"

She closed her eyes and threw back her head when she laughed this time, giving me the opportunity I needed. I snatched up the vase of flowers from the table and flung it at her, then raced around the settee toward the door. Marisol grabbed for me, hooked her fingers in my long skirt and yanked. I lost my balance and we tumbled to the floor, grappling for the gun. She was stronger than she looked and she fought as dirty as they come. I lost more than a fistful of hair, and her nails had raked my face and arms before I got hold of the derringer, clipped her on the chin with it and knocked her out.

I bound her to the bed frame with the drapery cords, then sat a moment to catch my breath before changing into my jeans and the torn ski parka. I grabbed my Glock and was halfway down the stairs, still wiping blood from my face, when the front door opened.

Sheriff Brady Pierce stood there, silent and suspicious, six shooter in hand, his eyes moving from my face to the Glock and back again.

"It's all about gold," I said when I was sure he wouldn't open fire. "Marisol and Jose. They kidnapped Amelia to make Florence forge property deeds in their name. She's being held at the old sawmill. Marisol's tied up upstairs," I nodded my head toward the ceiling without taking my eyes off his, "but Jose's not around. We have to get to Amelia before he finds out that we know, and kills her."

He stared at me a moment longer, his face clouded with hostility. Then his eyes cleared and he nodded.

"Let's go," he said, and led the way out to his horse.

We never did find Jose. For all Marisol's disdain of her brother's stupidity, he'd been smart enough to read the writing on the wallpaper and vanish into the night. We found Amelia, bound and gagged, in a small, dark storeroom at the back of the mill, about twelve miles from town. She was weak from abuse and hunger, and sporting enough bruises to show she'd put up a good fight, but claimed that Jose never had carried through on his threat to show her just what a woman was made for.

I watched her tearful reunion with her mother from the front porch, where I stood with Philip and Sheriff Pierce.

"They could have just walked away and let her die," Philip said, "and we'd never have known what happened to her." He squeezed my hand. "Thank you for finding her."

"An' it warn't worth it, anyways," the sheriff said. "That gold 'neath the ol' mill's jist a trace. Few hunnert dollers, maybe a thousand, that's all. If'n they'd asked about it, they'da saved themselves a passel 'a trouble."

He touched the scabbing scratches on my face, then tipped his hat and sauntered down the steps. Philip and I trailed behind him, heading for the cafe.

"Do you think they'll find Jose?" I asked, though I didn't really care. I just wanted to go home—my hundred-plus-years-in-the-future home.

"Probably back in Mexico by now, so I doubt it," Philip said with a smile. "But Marisol will be our 'guest' for quite a few years, since the forged deeds are in her name, and she masterminded the scheme. She—"

"Papa! *Bruja!*"

The high-pitched call echoed in the still night air. We turned to see little Joseph barreling toward us, waving his arms. Snow began to fall, a sudden heavy burst from what moments before had been a cloudless sky.

"Not *bruja*, Joseph," I said as the boy hugged me and stepped back. The wind began to howl and with what he was about to witness I wondered if he'd believe me. "Not magic, but—"

"—science!" we chanted together. I turned my head from the onslaught, shoulders hunched, eyes shut against the stinging cold. "Goodbye, Philip," I called.

And I spun away into the raging storm.

* * * *

"Hey, watch it!"

I whacked into a hard, bony body and landed in an icy pile of slush. My backside instantly froze and my breath shuddered in my lungs.

"Are you okay?" a hoarse male voice asked. "Are you hurt?"

I squinted against the brilliant sunshine at the man, who held out a huge paw to help me up.

"Crap!" I said, wiping slush and ice from my jeans, freezing my ungloved hands in the process. "I'm fine," I told him. "Just wet and cold. Sorry."

"Where in heaven did you come from, anyway?" he asked. He took off his sheepskin lined gloves and wool scarf and handed them to me. "Here, you need these more than I do."

"Thanks. And you wouldn't believe me if I told you." I looked around, saw Gorman's seedy motel a block and a half to my right and the MacLarren's place a block and a half to my left. "What's the date?" I asked my concerned Samaritan.

"Today? December fifteen. Opened the road just this morning. Most everyone's gone by now."

My heart began to thud.

"And the year?"

"You sure you're okay?" He squinted at me. "Same's it's been for 349 days. Twenty-ten."

"Thank you!" I said, to the man, the sunshine, the Universe. "Thank you." Then I took his name and address and promised to return his gloves and scarf.

He ambled off with a bemused expression, muttering about 'young people.' I was thrilled, at the ripe old age of twenty-eight, to be included in that category. Not until I started to follow him did I notice the sign, even though I'd almost landed on top of it.

In Memory of Amelia Sanchez
Native of Gorman, California
1863 — 1941
California's First Female Bank President
"Life's mysteries only make us stronger."

Good for you, Amelia, I thought as I headed back to the MacLarren's to dry my backside a bit before hitting the road for home. Much better to be known for your accomplishments than for being one of life's mysteries. I reached into my pocket for my cell. It wasn't there. I'd left it on the bedside table back in 1886, there to proclaim its "No Service" message until the battery ran down. I walked on, wondering if a twenty-first century anachronism was perhaps moldering away in a 124-year-old box in the MacLarren's attic. It could, I supposed, be considered both magic and science equally, depending on the year of discovery.

As for me? I thought about the psychic gifts I'd been cursed with, and where they'd led me this time. Then I thought about saving Amelia Sanchez, who'd gone on to make a significant mark in her world. And I decided that maybe my karma wasn't so bad after all.

◆ ◆ ◆ ◆

Susan Tuttle, a professional editor/writing coach, is the award-winning author of the suspense novel, *Tangled Webs*, available through bookstores, at Amazon, and on her website. Her work has appeared in the *SLO City News*, the *Coast News*, the *Bay News* and *MindPrints Literary Journal*. She is hard at work on the first volume of a new paranormal detective series featuring Skylark. Contact her through her websites: http://www.susant-creations.com and http://www.susant-writer.com, or on Facebook.

Captain of the Rags

Anne Schroeder

"Bellysticker. Dumpster-ripe. Rat bait." The Captain of the Rags screams his torment in the treeless canopy of neon where city and jungle collide. Tonight, the Viet Cong press close disguised as rats foraging in the litter of the sidewalk. Camouflaged in the filth, the Captain defends his territory with his rage. He hears a noise and his eyes sweep the perimeter where the enemy rustles in the shadows. "Bellysticker. Rat bait."

From further down the alley a bottle explodes against the darkened pavement, sending up a spray of glass shrapnel. With a flick, the Captain beds a knife handle into the curve of his hand and bends into a defensive stance, his back against the brick wall.

It is midnight. Already his eyes burn with exhaustion, but he dismisses the irritation with a swipe of his hand. The night will be long, his need for vigilance will be great because the moon is full and the crazies are out tonight. The time for sleeping will come with the sun.

As his echoes fade in the urban canyon, the bamboo forest fades into a confusion of battered trashcans and wooden crates. An illusion: in the crumbling brick alley nothing stays the same. The next moment he finds a glint of normalcy in the mundane. Relieved of his fear, he slips the knife back into its sheath, unbloodied, and swipes the sweat furrowing his brow. With shaking fingers he uncaps his Thunderbird wine and drinks greedily, feeling the tremors ease. Enough for now, save some for later. He waits until he is sure that no one watches, then pulls two loose bricks from the wall and shoves his bottle into the cleft. His secret safe, he turns toward the late-night traffic to begin his night patrol.

The door to the thrift store is locked, as it is every night, blocked by bags and boxes of discarded rummage. He unleashes his fury on the scarred sheet-metal, but the door does not give. The voices in his head are back, blocking street sounds. *Dominos Vobiscum. Pater Nostrum. Shut the hell up. Hallelujah, stick it all. Kill the messenger.* Sometimes he mumbles the words, sometimes the voices whisper secrets to confound the enemy and he must obey. Tonight they are confused. Wild-eyed, he backs behind a heaping cardboard box and claims it. Blocking it from another scavenger who threatens his find, he stands with arms widespread, a buzzard hoarding its carrion.

"Move over, you crazy derelict." For a moment he doesn't connect the words with the speaker, but he recognizes the crone who snatches a child's purple sweater from under his arm. He growls in warning and she retreats, mewling like a cat. He savors the feeling of triumph, but the sensation is fleeting, replaced by the familiar pain that dogs his days.

The Captain of the Rags has no need of the garment—any more than for the throbbing molar in his left jaw. Survival screams to him through the pain, but this piddling irritation is nothing to what will come when the winter makes hard knots in his legs. For now he has wine to keep his tremors at bay, but he dreads the times when he returns to reality, knife in hand, when nothing makes sense. The foreboding makes his skin crawl. He has learned to speak only when the voices demand it. Right now they are silent.

Crouched on a heap of bundled cardboard, he dumps the box onto the blacktop. A sign on the back door reads *NO DUMPING*. It is only midnight. Already five boxes and half a dozen grocery bags litter the steps. He kicks one and it ruptures, spilling torn tee shirts with faded logos, undershorts with stretched elastic, polyester men's trousers splattered with dried paint. The other bags show no better—people who leave their castoffs in the cover of darkness know the value of their gift. The rich are no better than the alley rats in this—they drop their boxes and scuttle off into the night before others can see the value of their leavings. *For the needy*—a bastardization of fact, he thinks—useful for people who would lose their way without it.

Inside his head an enemy battalion of social workers and politicians battle church ladies with kettles of chicken soup. *For the homeless.* Home is a state of mind, a matter for the voices. They tell him when to move.

In the alley, other hands sort through his pile. Molly, pockmarked hag with a crippled leg, has her grocery cart half filled. The Captain swipes to cuff her across the belly, misses, and is satisfied that she moves back a few paces. Despite his growl, he is glad that she moves. He has no fight left for women. "Dammed rag picker." The voices persist and he speaks for them. "Maybe she is. Shut up." He will not shut up. He will be silent if it suits him. He will not be hurried. He finds a boot, Red Wing, size ten. He passes his index finger through a crevice where the welt should be attached. Squinting, he studies the boot's run-over heels. "Speed, speed bitch." Molly tosses the boot's mate in his direction. "Ahoy matey." The voices grumble; *Long enough. Why bother? Thirsty, thirsty.*

Deliberately, he ties the ends of the laces together and hangs the pair over his shoulder like a brace of newly felled pheasants. A good find, reminiscent of field hunts and shotguns, tools of the past when hunting was a sport, when his father and grandfather, three generations, crossed the field on a crisp autumn morning and the steam rose off the straw rows.

A vision encroaches, of mist pouring off rice paddies and filling the jungle, and the memory is ruined. He sweeps the ground for hidden mines as he stumbles to the next set of boxes. Once he found a real overcoat when its Jew owner stumbled and fell against the curb. The man didn't need the coat any longer. He grabbed it before the ambulance came, and spent the winter warm. The coat had the owner's initials stitched on the inside, LMB. Wool, mohair, silk. He'd seen silkworms in 'Nam. Run Rat tried to grab it off his back one night, but Rat wouldn't cause trouble in the camps anymore.

The Captain wouldn't bury his knife, but he laid low until the cops stopped looking—four, five weeks. They let him be now, for the most part. He was getting too old to interest the cops. The county didn't want to pen up old guys anyway, not when their teeth were bad and they coughed up yellow phlegm.

"Stick it. Stay away from my eye. Angels, too many angels. Fallen angels. Why do you care?" Tonight his head holds a picture of Sara Michelle, his child. She was seven last time he saw her. Be a good thing if she stayed that way. Life is hard on women. Better if she stayed skinny, long braids, book smart. When he closes his eyes he sees her smile. Better that he left when he did—when the voices started screaming about her. He tried to forget the name of the town where she lived with her mother. Tried to forget them both. It was better that his child think he was dead, the story he agreed to with the mother. Better for all of them.

Someone is listening to his voices. "You'd be better off dead, damn bum." A bundled voice walking a dog brings him from his head.

Thoughts of his child have made him careless. He growls his warning before he has time to think. "Good coat, man. You be dead, you won't need a thing like that." He watches, undecided, as his fingers twitch against his blade.

He takes two steps in pursuit before his legs begin trembling. Behind him the others ransack the boxes and paper bags. They will be witnesses if it comes to violence, not all of them to be trusted. Someone would tell the police if it comes to that. *Whatthehell*....

The voices demand to be warmer. In the street a pile of dead leaves sits where a boy has raked them. He sinks onto the heap and strips a leaf, uses its cellulose vein to probe his tender gums while the headlights of the street sweeper turn the corner. When it is a car-length away he scrambles to the curb and watches the machine roar past. The driver will laugh to his friends at the end of his shift about the damned bum he almost ran over, but the Captain of the Rags is no dog in the street. He covers his head with his hands and tries to block out the words. "Getthehell out. Beggar wine."

A scrap of red plaid flutters from the dumpster. He grabs the frayed cuff just as One-Eye snatches it. "Drop it or I'll fill the damned box with your brains." He leaves the knife sheathed when the guy scurries away like a cellar rat. One-Eye is no soldier he would want on his patrol, a coward who has left the shirt behind without a fight.

The Captain presses the shirt against his lips. The wool is scratchy: smells of ewes and shearing pens, conjures a memory of his grandfather's farm and the thought eases his pain. The label, LL Bean—in small green letters—brings a crinkle to his eyes. American made. Too much waste, foreign goods—clothes made for a season, not even worth picking up. He squints to read the label and recalls the chino trousers he found in the trash behind the Sears and Roebuck, zipper broken, but flannel lined. They eased his knotted veins against the wind for a winter—until the cops trampled them in the mud the night they raided the willow camp with flashlights and dogs. The catarrh in his throat threatens to choke him.

From out of the darkness a stranger approaches, the pattern of the footfalls unfamiliar, someone not to be trusted. Sure enough, the stranger threatens. "Get outahere bum or I'll call the cops."

The Captain ignores the security guard and the beam from his flashlight, and spits a wad of yellow phlegm onto the concrete while Molly stuffs a child's pink party dress into her grocery cart and scuttles away. He has a few minutes before the cops arrive. He grabs a handful of wool socks, stuffs a single gray one into his frayed overcoat. His hand catches on the torn pocket of his button-less coat. It used to be warm but he stripped the lining to wrap his arm when someone slashed it with a broken bottle. He still owns the ragged scar, but the ER nurse tossed the lining away as if it were nothing. He searched for it afterwards, but the hospital dumpster frightened the voices.

A black and white turns the corner. He slips between two buildings and takes a whiz in the alley. His body warmed by the new shirt, his blood is warmed by the encounter and his thoughts are calm.

Winter is coming. He can smell the stink of charity in the loose change when he panhandles uptown. By mid-winter when he could use a hot meal and pocket money, people are back in their houses, their charitable notions, forgotten. But for five weeks everyone is Santa Claus. They toss their change in the Salvation Army buckets and walk past the panhandlers without seeing their faces, and the soup kitchen lines grow long. Feast or famine. By Christmas he can hardly swallow another bite of turkey, would give anything for a slice of ham or roast beef, but choice is not his concern. Enough to expect that it fill the hole in his belly. Sometimes the voices tell him to drink his supper.

"Get a life, you jerk." The security guard yells from the corner as the black and white cruises past.

The worst are the damned red mittens that the canteen workers hand out on Christmas Eve. Last year he traded his for a bottle of something that would keep him warmer. A men's store behind the synagogue sometimes throws out a glove or two when the stitches work loose and some rich bastard returns them. Tonight he squints at his greasy, mismatched pair, and his chuckle erupts into a racking cough. Maybe he can get his money back. Test the guarantee.

Laughter comes hard—a chortle when he can spare it—but this time the cough won't stop and the wool sock slips unnoticed from his pocket. His gut feels like it belongs to one of the guys he used to load onto gurneys for a one-way chopper ride to the rear in 'Nam—like he is bleeding to death without the blood. When he can breathe again he moves out of the wind. "Gotta keep moving. Damn it all. Colors. Why not colors. Mother bitch. Keep it."

The moon makes the night hard and he walks the sidewalks to keep the demons at bay. Near the Temple Beth Shalom he crouches in an alcove where the building breaks the wind. Steam rises from a heating grate near the stairwell. No one else is around; he holds the spot tonight, squatter's rights. "Don't eat. Never, never. Watch out. Kill for golden air."

The parking lot empties except for a single car. The building's lights go dark. He hears a door slam, followed by a quick tap, tap, tap. It is the rabbi, a pasty-faced rabbit of a man who likes to hold a voucher for a Big Mac and a cup of coffee just out of reach while he quotes scripture. Some of the others will take it, sit up and beg like a dog, but not him. A man who has never had the shakes has no business holding back another man's meal. The rabbi can go to his hell.

Something shifts in his brain, maybe the moon's pull on his sanity, maybe just the need for another drink. Hatred builds in the pit of his stomach, sour, like bile after one of his blackouts. *Take him, kill, kill. He's the crazy one. You, you're the one. Kill the bastard. Shut up.* He crouches on all fours, shaking his nappy mane from side to side while the voices argue. He palms his knife handle and slides it from its sheath. As he stands, his Red Wings make a soft brushing sound against the cement.

Slowly the rabbi turns. He wears an overcoat, its buttons sewed with waxed thread so that they will never come off.

Watch the eyes. The Captain waits for the fear, but there is none. Instead, the eyes speak to him, another voice in the confusion. Grave and watchful, the eyes hold a soft expression of sorrow that seems to accept death's right but regrets its necessity. The rabbi makes no move to run or to offer defense. Without one or the other, the voices are confused. Their arguments tighten in his head until he screams for silence. The voices obey and he raises his knife.

The rabbi's nerve disintegrates in a zigzagging race across the juniper clogging the median.

Crouching, the Captain gives chase. The jungle chokes on moonlight as the landscaper's spikes tear through the webbing of his boot. Too late, he remembers the damned gooks and their bamboo. He opens his mouth and lunatic rage fills the air with blasphemous, God-damning oaths. In a scream of pain he falls hard onto the concrete.

Black fog blots his vision. Something has gone wrong. Blood runs down to his boots and for once his belly is warm. But his instincts tell him that something is out of place in the battle. The enemy is confused, the wrong foe has caught the slice. The pain tells him everything—more than he wants to know.

In the distance he hears the sound of honking cars and laughter. From his throat a dog snarls its fury. The throbbing of his temples silences the voices; they are dead, waiting to die. Blood-blind, he rakes the darkness for his knife, his stubbed fingers scraping the cement with a hollow, rasping sound. His fingers probe the fire in his belly and he feels the bayonet in his ribs.

A sound behind him: the rabbi stands, crooning prayers in a lilting voice that brings tears to both of them. This time there is no sermon. The Captain watches bright red foam bubbling from his lung. His spittle feels thick, like the cement. Everything is warm. No, even without the voices he knows he is wrong; the sidewalk is cold. His body convulses like a soldier with shrapnel in his gut while his blood eases through the holes in his coat.

Above him the rabbi casts a shadow from the streetlight. He shrugs out of his overcoat and drapes it onto the Captain of the Rags.

The Captain feels the weight, recalls the scent of shearing pens and bleating ewes, fresh shorn, with bleeding nicks from the shearing blade. The jungle fades, taking with it the enemy. In its place his father's lambing barn sits at the edge of the rolling pasture. In the distance a horn honks.

The bass warning resonates in his brain, free; the voices have retreated. Blood trickles to his groin, hot against his body. The hitch of wool and mohair against his neck traps his heat. It is good, waiting warm. Hearing the rabbi's prayers.

♦ ♦ ♦ ♦

Anne Schroeder writes women's fiction and memoir, including published memoirs: *Branches on the* Conejo and *Ordinary Aphrodite*; essays on the woman's experience. Her fiction has appeared in over forty magazines and she is currently working on a woman's novel. Anne lives in Atascadero with her husband of 43 years. http://www.readanneschroeder.com.

Bal Masque

Eileen Dunbaugh

Patches of green could be seen all across the Hudson Highlands that mild January, as the land bounded suggestively down to the river, its curves matched by a contrary sweep of majesty—like a woman ambiguously inviting or scorning. There lay the heart of the problem for the newcomer, William Belmare, who strutted across the porch of the small mansion he'd wrested from one of the valley's oldest families: Would he be accepted into the embrace of this seductive place—its society and politics no less than the earth he'd need to see a yield from—or meet with haughty rejection?

He felt in his pocket and pulled out a cigar, lit it, and exhaled his doubts with the plume of smoke. This first hour of possession was a time for exultation. In his breast pocket, next to his fast-beating heart, were the papers to the property, deeded by the crown, in colonial times, to the original Livingstons.

His Livingston had owned but a small portion of the original acreage, and didn't bear the illustrious name—but he bore the blood, and that was enough for Belmare. He would expand the house to equal in elegance the best estates in the valley.

Roused by that ambition, he tore his gaze away from the coiling river.

* * * *

Down the curving drive, another man trod steadily towards him. His posture and stride betrayed nothing of his temper, for Matthew Borne was a man who kept his emotions to himself.

Borne didn't need a closer view to know what manner of landlord Belmare would be. His reputation had preceded him, the whispered word traveling from the kitchens and stables of the great estates with wondrous speed, like Samuel Morse's telegraph, the valley's latest marvel.

The old families despised Belmare: a *parvenu,* the ladies murmured to each other, and their maids, tenant farm girls all, flew like pigeons to their familial roosts, bearing the gossip. The men were no more discreet: a trumped-up dandy who'd made his money in the fevered railway boom in England, trading in *stocks!* they grumbled in front of stable hands, as if those retainers had no deeper concerns than the soaping of saddles. As if, Borne ruminated, they weren't young men from the farms, who'd till their own soil and light fires under their own roofs if land were available.

Borne looked up from his reflections to see Belmare hoist a musket into his arms and swagger to the edge of the porch, tall and lean in plaid trousers and waistcoat.

So, Borne thought, *he has caught the scent of danger, knows the riots are moving down the valley, has heard of the sheriff's men, sent to collect rents, assaulted and injured near Albany.*

Borne slowed. He, almost alone of his class, had stood aloof from the armed bands of men in sheepskin, disdaining to disguise himself with hood or war paint and be branded a "Calico Indian."

Belmare let the musket drop a little. He knew the square man before him must be one of his tenants, but he'd come too soon to suit Belmare's plans; the lawyer with the details of the leases would not arrive till afternoon.

"Be off!" he shouted. "You'll be summoned in good time."

Borne came to a halt. "I've not come about the lease," he said, his gaze sweeping the house's deteriorating facade. "You'll be needing help, won't ye?"

Belmare was tempted, but if the insurrection spread, this wasn't the kind of man he wanted within his walls. Let him roam about and a dropped candle might, by seeming accident, burn the place to the ground.

He set the butt of his musket down, and waved Borne up the porch steps. "I need a *woman* of work," he acknowledged. "Someone to keep house and—"

"My name's Borne," the other interrupted him. "And you must be Squire Belmare. It's a housekeeper you need, eh?" He scratched his chin. "Emily Talley may be willing. She's a widow of some years. I'd not send a younger woman here."

"What is it you say?!" Belmare loomed towards him.

"It's a matter of simple decency, sir, which you'll do well to regard," said Borne calmly. "For what is talked of on the farms makes its way to the estates."

With that, Borne, who'd felt the calculation in Belmare's grudging civility, turned and started back the way he had come.

"About the leases." He turned back to Belmare. "In good time, you say. Good time is before the planting. There's some won't abide not knowing where they stand before the seed goes in the ground."

Belmare watched Borne turn his back on him and plod evenly toward the road, as if he'd merely uttered a statement of fact and not a threat more chill than the wind that suddenly came up from the shimmering river.

* * * *

Two months later, could he have been a fly on the wall, Belmare might have heard the answer to the question that had tormented him as he stood surveying his new domain.

"What is it?" the youngest Van Allen girl wheedled, reaching out to touch the envelope in her sister's hand.

"Something not to be opened till Mama is home."

"But it's addressed to Madame *and* Mesdemoiselles Van Allen."

"As if that did not speak ill enough of the sender."

A third sister lounged on a window seat which lent the room, with its French antiques and hand-painted wallpaper, a delicate coziness. The Van Allen mansion exhibited a restraint that had not been replicated in Belmare's designs for his house. The Van Allen girls did not know that yet, and one of them could hardly contain her curiosity. From her perch she pretended to study the movements of a doe across the meadow, while her eyes slid sideways to the letter in her sister's lap.

"What do you think it is, Grace?" the youngest girl asked her.

"I think it must be an invitation. And I think *you*, Mary, are unfair," she said to the custodian of the letter. She stretched as if the matter was of no consequence to her and crossed to take a seat near the others. "The man would like to know his neighbors, and the house is finished. They say he employed half the carpenters in Poughkeepsie. The architect's a city man, of course."

When Mary replied with a disapproving look, she continued:

"Most of the best families have gone to Manhattan, you know. But they'll be returning now the weather's fine. I imagine Mr. Belmare—"

"How come *you* to know so much about the man?"

"I know what Gertrude says."

"Ah. A maid and her gossip! That's what you fill your head with, Grace?"

"I believe her; her aunt is William Belmare's housekeeper. And word can travel as quickly in the other direction," she warned, as she spotted a skirt under the door to the hall.

* * * *

Across that hall, the father of "Mesdemoiselles Van Allen" had reasons to take issue with Belmare that had nothing to do with the man's approach to his daughters—a circumstance concerning which he as yet knew nothing.

"Beirstin was a fool!" he roared to his son Jasper. "He should have evicted his tenants, if it came to that. He's brought a blight upon the whole valley by selling to a man like that!"

"He didn't exactly *sell* the place to Belmare, Father. Not in the way you suggest. He'd taken a loan and used the estate as security. Would you really have had him seize his tenants' houses and barns? The temper of the times won't stand for it."

"The *temper of the times*. Is that the kind of nonsense comes out of John Bull these days?"

"The change is coming, Father, whether we like it or not. The anti-rent faction will have its own legislators soon. And there are rumblings in Europe of much deeper discontent. I brought some writings home for you. There's a tract you should pay particular attention to, by a man called Marx—"

"Save your tracts for idlers like yourself," the elder Van Allen thundered. "If there's discontent in England, they've only themselves to blame. They're the ones who made trumped-up millionaires of men like Belmare, with their endless speculation on railways that are never built—"

"Many a true gentleman has entered into *that* game, Father, even if they conceal it under cover of an agent."

"They'll live to regret it, mark my words. There's nothing to support it, just pieces of paper. . . . But that's not why I wanted to see you, Jasper." He dabbed with his handkerchief at the spittle that had spewed from his mouth. "That jackanape Belmare has made up a new lease; he's requiring his tenants to plant more of the land."

"So? Why trouble yourself about his affairs?"

"Why?" The elder Van Allen raised his fist. "Because should the yield be good, he'll drive prices down for us all!"

"Bah, Father. He hasn't sufficient acreage."

"Not alone, perhaps; but I have it on good authority that Kessler and Romijn have got themselves into debt to him too, and that Belmare will call the notes unless they follow suit."

"Why then, ignore them all. In a few years they'll exhaust their soil and our farms will have the advantage."

"What a fool I've made of you, Jasper, with your tracts and your—your— *frilly* cravats." He waved a disgusted hand in the direction of his son's sartorial excess. "Why do you think so many of our farmers are in arrears, eh? Already they're barely able to compete with the rye shipping through the canal—

"Ah, never mind. What you don't know would fill the whole length of the Erie from Albany to Buffalo. But I tell you this: Should the price for rye fall further, in two years we'll be in Beirstin's position. And it's *Belmare* who'll buy our land."

"But you have a plan. I see it in your face."

"Aye," the senior Van Allen said. "There's a man name of Borne, a tenant on Belmare's estate. I hear most look to him to say whether to accept Belmare's terms. Borne has stayed away from the rallies. If he could be made to refuse Belmare—even better, if he could be made to throw his lot in with those ruffians— those "Indians—"

"By God, you can't be serious!"

"Ah, but I am. They'll soon overstep themselves; the governor won't allow this to go on much longer. And if, in the meantime, Belmare can be frightened—"

"That's a dangerous game, Father—and foolish. Besides, who would you have recruit this Borne?"

"Ah. Now *that* is the matter we must consider . . . "

* * * *

While father and son pondered the problem of how to snare Borne, the Van Allen daughters were occupied with the letter that Mrs. Van Allen, who'd been drawn immediately into their midst on arriving home, held open in her hand.

"A masked ball? Here? In the country?"

"He's built a ballroom in the addition," Grace said. And to the question that brought to the stern eyes of her mother, "So Gertrude says."

"Well, you'll have to leave that and all the other appointments of the house to your imaginations, my dears. We *will not* go!"

"What is it that has you so indignant, Mrs. Van Allen?" said the elder Van Allen as he and Jasper entered the room. With a pull on the bell to summon Gertrude with tea, he turned his attention to his wife.

"That man. The one who took Beirstin's place. He's having a masked ball—a *bal masque,* he calls it. He has written to me, and has addressed his invitation to your daughters too, Mr. Van Allen."

The color rose in the senior Van Allen's face. A "gentleman"—which, for him, meant one of Manhattan's "upper ten"—did not address young ladies of family without first seeking the acceptance of their fathers—oh no. And Van Allen, who spent most of his time on his country estate, far from the predations of the new city men, the money-manipulators like Belmare, had never entertained the thought that a brazen approach might be made to his own brood.

Gertrude came in with the tea, concealing the tiny smile that played about her lips. She'd heard enough to know that her aunt's misdirection had worked. There'd be no Van Allens attending Belmare's ball.

She looked up from setting out the cups and saucers and saw the elder Van Allen start to sputter some reply to the outrage Belmare had perpetrated, then pause as if touched by the Almighty Himself, pace, and finally, a sly look coming over his countenance, he turned his stocky body to Mrs. Van Allen. "You will accept, my dear. What is the theme of the ball, pray?"

Mrs. Van Allen's head bobbed in confusion, like a bird presented with an uncrackable nut. "But Mr. Van Allen, to go there . . . what will people say?"

"You can be sure the Kesslers and Romijns will be there. What is the theme, I say."

"Marie Antoinette. We are asked to go in the style," she murmured, "of Marie Antoinette."

Shrill laughter squeezed itself through Van Allen's throat. "Ah," he said, "how fortunate. *La Revolution* would not be complete without someone to play the executioner now, would it?"

At the words, Gertrude sent a cup shattering to the floor.

* * * *

At the Talley farm that night, pipes were lit and heads gathered round. Closest to the fire sat broad Emily Talley, housekeeper to William Belmare, relating how she'd intervened in a flirtation observed from a window of Belmare's house on a blustery day a month past. First there'd been only the girl, making her way along the river path high above the water, the large bell of her skirt caught from underneath by the wind, so that it whooped up and fell down like a bouncing ball. It was her bonnet that betrayed her, though. She must not have had it tied properly, for as Emily watched, it flew off and tumbled, then rolled swiftly ahead of her until it crossed the path to which Belmare had descended, intent on seeing how his house would appear to riverboats plying upstream from New York.

Stripped of her bonnet, the walker was recognizable to Emily as Grace Van Allen. When she sighted Belmare, the girl stopped dead in her tracks. From the formal bow he proffered as he handed back the bonnet, Emily concluded it was their first meeting. Innocent enough, until Grace composed herself and gestured at the house, and Belmare urged her farther down the path. Perhaps, Emily thought, Grace had only come out for air, but there was a restlessness about that middle Van Allen daughter that made Emily uneasy. Should she tarry there again, Emily decided, she would devise some way of putting an end to it.

And that, she explained, was how she came to advise Belmare to include a direct address to the Van Allen daughters in his invitation to the ball. Whatever others might say, Emily had found Belmare malleable, constantly appealing to her regarding the rules of behavior of the fine folk, which Emily knew from having once been secretary to the Romijns.

But now here was Gertrude, surprising them with the news that the Van Allens would attend the ball.

Emily's brother tapped the ash out of his pipe and said, "Something must be done. Such a marriage would bring him into the fold."

"I'll *not* interfere further," declared Emily. "I've meddled enough. You heard Gert say there was an evil look in Master Van Allen's eye. There'll be trouble, and I bear my share o' blame for stirring the pot—"

As if to confirm her prediction, there came the sound of horses and a knocking at the door, which was let open to reveal two men in soiled cotton shirts and fustian breeches, faces flushed and splattered from the mush of spring roads. "There's to be a meeting at Matthew Borne's, tomorrow night," one said, after nodding his greetings to the assembled.

"About Belmare?" George Talley challenged. "He be n't *our* landlord."

"Be n't your landlord *yet,*" the other returned. "Andrew Merthen, at Van Allen's, heard the master say Belmare's proposal is a trick. He'll have all the acreage farmed, break our backs and overburden the soil, all to drive the owners he cannot control to ruin. And then, says Van Allen, once Belmare's bought up more land, he'll seize everything his tenants have."

George stood and surveyed the faces of the other Talleys. Emily sat still and thoughtful: Only a man content to be hated pursued such a course, and Belmare, who inspected his teeth every time he passed a mirror, was not such a one. The peacock sought admiration, not hatred, she thought; but this was not the time to say so.

* * * *

Matthew Borne, too, sat deep in contemplation that night. The riders had come and gone, and Matthew's natural skepticism turned to scrutinizing every part of their story. Why should Van Allen have that conversation in particular—one concerning Belmare's *tenants*—where his stable hand could hear? It hinted of calculation more than accident to Borne. As if Van Allen wanted to incite them against the new man.

"Go to bed," he said to his wife, whose flesh jiggled as she reached across him to pick up his empty glass.

"It's but two weeks till the rye's to be seeded. You've decided, have ye, whether to accept Belmare's terms?" she said.

"I have not," her husband replied.

"For Catherine's sake, Matthew—" she began, for the good wife of Matthew Borne knew that should they refuse Belmare they'd no choice but to face down the rent collectors.

"I've no need to be told to consider Catherine." Borne cut her off. His daughter claimed a fond place in his heart, as all knew from the small gifts he lavished upon her. "Whatever I decide," he said, his tone softening, "if there's trouble, the authorities will look to me for cause. You know that, Bess?"

She did; many an hour before dawn she'd awakened with the terror of it upon her. A man who will not put his heart on display may command, without trying, the respect of other men. But for the respect some men bore him, others, equally, feared and despised him.

Borne sat in the light of an oil lamp, the fire extinguished, long after Bess had gone to her restless bed. The sheltering walls, bent to fantastic angles by the lamp flame, had been erected by a Borne four score years ago. He would not see them sold on, with his lease, to a farmer come from abroad. The question was only whether he'd keep hold of what was his by adding his torch to the Indians' or wait for the legislature to abolish the system of unjust tenancy that threatened them with removal.

* * * *

While Borne mulled his bitter choices, William Belmare was reveling in acceptances to his *bal masque*. The following morning, he towered over Emily Talley, smoking his cigar, as she read the names of those she proposed to employ as temporary maids, cooks, and footmen. At "Catherine Borne" Belmare gave a small start, but grunted his approval before Emily could notice his discomfort. He had not forgotten the chill that teased at him on first meeting Borne, nor Borne's refusal, so far, to comment on the terms he had put forth for the leases.

But Belmare had more pleasant thoughts to turn to than Borne. His acquaintance with Grace Van Allen had progressed from seeking the young lady's approval of his terraces to admiring her dress and, by their third "chance" encounter, to his complimenting her on the "snowy marble" of her complexion and the "ermine" of her hair. His shopworn praise might have cooled Grace's growing warmth had her sap not been running so high; but all around the birds of air and beasts of field were wriggling in spring coitus and her own skin burned for a touch by a hand that smelled of tobacco and leather.

Belmare's lust was more for the satisfaction of his vanity than for the joys of the flesh, but Grace Van Allen presented an opportunity to satisfy both. When she'd gone so far as to accept a quick brush across the lips, he suggested—to protect her reputation, of course—a more private place of assignation. Neither proposed that Belmare apply to her father, for both knew it would bring closer scrutiny upon them.

And so it was with stealth that Belmare slipped away from his housekeeper and down the river path.

"She walks in beauty, like the night/ Of cloudless climes and starry skies" he read aloud from a small volume as he turned into the meeting place, a small embrasure in the cliff face. The words were *in apropos* of both the sunny day and the fact that, far from walking, the young lady was crouched in a most uncomfortable fashion upon a rock. But he had no need to be concerned about the words, for Grace, on seeing him enter with the open book, felt the blood rush to her face in embarrassment and confusion. She could not have given voice to her sudden awareness that it was a mistake to be there with the verse-spouting Belmare, but she felt it profoundly.

Belmare took her rise in color, her confusion of speech, as signs of passion, and, dispensing with the book, sat down close beside her and put his arm around her waist. At the touch, Grace felt another kind of heat suffuse her, and like a rabbit caught trembling and witless in the coils of a snake, not knowing how to extricate herself, she yielded to his embrace.

When it was over, Belmare said, "We must elope; there's nothing else to be done." And with that he helped her onto the path, pulled out a cigar, and lit it with satisfaction. "We must meet here tomorrow and make our plans."

* * * *

The evening of the ball was cloudless and starry, like those immortalized in the poem by Byron that Belmare had read to Grace. The music of a small orchestra playing a Verdi overture drifted out to the portico where Belmare—attired as Louis XVI; silk pantaloons, white stockings, crown, and fur-trimmed robe of blue and gold—stood watching the carriages come up the drive. The belle of the ball, had there been one he could acknowledge, would have come as Marie Antoinette. But Belmare had warned Grace that she must not, by costume or manner, cut herself out for observation or comment. Their plan depended on it.

The first carriage to arrive belonged to the Romijns, and when they had debarked, the lady of that name, garbed as the famous queen, took her place beside Belmare in the vestibule of the refurbished mansion. Her husband, whose debts to Belmare were mounting, had persuaded her to assume the role.

When the Van Allens were announced, led by the elder Van Allen clad in boots, riding britches, a workman's shirt, and black executioner's hood, Belmare caught his breath. The certainty that Van Allen had discovered the affair with Grace and was signaling his intent to avenge it turned his bowels to jelly. Only Grace could have let that secret out. Relieved, he saw that next in the party were two dressed as ladies in waiting, their trains upheld by two others of feminine figure clad in the plain clothes of serving girls—one of the latter recognizable to Belmare, from the outturned placing of her feet, as Grace.

* * * *

Two hours later, twenty couples whirled happily in a waltz, the abandon of this modern dance, thought Emily Talley, at variance with their costumes, which begged for a dignified quadrille. The young of that time preferred to waltz, and Belmare, still a young man himself, had directed the orchestra to play only four quadrilles, and then to liven the rest of the evening with dances that were the mode in Europe.

Emily watched to see if Belmare paid particular attention to Grace Van Allen, or if Grace's eye should wander to him, but he danced with her only once.

Emily would have felt a measure of satisfaction for Belmare, for she liked the childish hopefulness beneath his grasping exterior, had she not known what was coming.

When the orchestra began a polka, she realized the moment was near, and looked around. She could warn Belmare, at least, not to venture outside. She *must*. But he was nowhere to be seen.

The dancers cavorted about the floor without the faintest inkling that the ground beneath them would soon quake from more than their stomping feet.

Alarm clouded Emily's searching eyes. Where was Belmare?

She slipped down the hall to the outer door, looked around and off to her right, and saw two figures running. One was Belmare. And with him? . . . Oh, surely not!

The ground began to tremble slightly. There were pinpoints of light in the distance that she knew to be torches. The running pair must have felt the hoof beats too, for they turned to look where Emily stared—where whoops like war cries now distantly teased the air as the horsemen drove on.

Belmare ran for a horse tethered outside the stable, pulling his companion roughly with him.

The hoof beats rose to a crescendo, and the massed shapes took form in the dark. In vain Emily shouted out the names of those she knew.

The first Indians were upon Belmare and the woman before Belmare could ride off, their numbers so thick Emily could see little of what happened.

As she scuttled for the house, her heart near to beating out of her chest, from among the throng surrounding Belmare, some now dismounted, a man in black hood and workman's clothes rushed forward with the screech of a wildcat, cudgel raised, to swing wildly at Belmare. A shorter and squarer man than Belmare, the attacker's reach fell short of the crowned head, but Belmare soon fell, and more blows of the club broke the writhing victim's legs and arms.

The crack of bone and splatter of blood caused many of the Indians to turn their neighing and snorting mounts away.

Soon men poured from the house armed with muskets, and in the space of an owl's hoot, it seemed to Emily, the horsemen disappeared, leaving Belmare lying in a puddle of blood.

Sides beginning to stitch, Emily ran into the stables searching for the woman.

Perplexed but relieved, she found no sign of another party to Belmare's designs.

* * * *

The attempted murder of William Belmare, being also a political crime, was brought to the attention of the Governor at

Albany. The fact that Belmare, who has not expected to recover, still breathed, did little to slow the wheels of justice.

Two of the most fervent of the Indians, so brave in their war paint, waned cowardly when threatened with the noose and turned on Matthew Borne, testifying that it was a hooded man of his stature who delivered the blows.

When the sheriff's men came for him, Borne was calm, stating simply that it was not he who struck the blows; he'd ridden with the Indians at the back of the throng, his mare too restive to move closer in.

Speaking loudest against him was the fact that Belmare had been seen with a masked woman the size of Borne's daughter Catherine, who'd served in Belmare's kitchen that night. Upon spying his daughter in the grip of a man who'd despoil but never marry her, Borne, a man reputed to have pent-up reserves of emotion, had been seized with a brutal rage: Such was the motive attributed to the crime.

The gallows was already being erected outside Poughkeepsie's stone jail. Borne could hear its planks being hammered into place from the tiny cell with mattress and stool in which he passed his hours reading a book brought to him by a sorrowful Catherine, whose word had not been taken that she'd had nothing to do with Belmare.

Borne might have been hanged had Belmare's heart not continued to beat, despite the contrary prognostications of his physicians.

It was on the fifth day of suspense over Belmare's life that a quaking Emily Talley took a ferry across the river and rode the coach to Albany, where she sat in the governor's anteroom until she succeeded in gaining an audience. Stalwart beneath her trembling, she swore that she herself had heard Matthew Borne tell the gathered Indians to be patient, that the law would soon change.

He'd ridden with them, she asserted, to temper any violence that erupted.

And then she related what she'd seen of Grace Van Allen and Belmare on the river path, told what Grace had been wearing the night of the ball—clothes indistinguishable, in the dark, from the frock of Catherine Borne. Told too how Grace's father, of similar build to Borne, had worn a black executioner's hood, workmen's clothes, riding boots.

To the official's savage retort that Van Allen had been inside the Belmare mansion, not outside consorting with ruffians, Emily rallied her courage again and declared that the servants would testify otherwise. She went further and insisted that the Indians' plan to interrupt the ball could be traced back to Van Allen himself, who'd talked repeatedly, in front of his stable hand, of the need to disrupt the dance and teach Belmare a lesson.

Emily Tally never found work with any of the old families again, but she let the authorities know that if they brought Borne to trial, the name Van Allen would be dragged down with him.

* * * *

If you're from these parts, you know how it ended, for the story's been passed down these many years. Belmare lived. Recovered to stride his way through the world again, albeit with a painful limp. The governor ordered the sheriff to drop all charges against Borne for the assault, but sentenced him to a long term in the drearest of prisons for inciting a riot.

Belmare claimed to have no recollection of the night of his beating, and threatened to go to law against anyone who slandered him with talk of a woman. By the autumn of that year 1845, he had, alas, no money for lawyering. The great English stock bubble on which he'd made his fortune burst and he was forced to sell everything.

Borne had been right that the legislature would deliver change. The day of the great landlords created by the crown drew to a close, their acreage bought by their tenant farmers. The day of the moneymen and captains of industry, on the other hand, was just beginning.

Van Allen, to his loss, lacked Borne's foresight; he'd been ignorant that Grace carried a baby sired by Belmare and might have claimed his name—a name that would become a byword in the Gilded Age to come. For Belmare sprang back before long, as moneymen do, making another fortune in another speculation.

Poor Grace. Belmare'd had a parson waiting to marry them at a chapel down the road; had planned to return to the ball before the last waltz was danced and confront Van Allen with the *fait accompli*. Grace might have become a great old lady of New York society, as he became one of its grand old men. But a man doesn't marry the daughter of his attempted murderer.

And the Bornes? Mother and daughter could not afford the farm alone, and went to work in a factory. Borne had shrunk to a grizzled stump of a man by the time he finally walked into the light beyond his prison door.

So much for the predictions of that fellow Marx, whose tract had found its way to young Jasper Van Allen. It's the rich, not the poor, who've risen up. You can see that in this year of 1900. Why, they've subdued even the valley herself. She'll not turn a haughty shoulder to the likes of Vanderbilt or her newest man, Rockefeller.

◆ ◆ ◆

Eileen Dunbaugh's first short story, "The Letter," appeared in the Mystery Writers of America anthology *The Prosecution Rests*, edited by Linda Fairstein, in 2009. Her story "A Poet's Justice" will appear in September of 2011 in *Murder New York Style: Fresh Slices*, an anthology of stories by members of the NY Tri-State Chapter of Sisters in Crime. "Bal Masque" was inspired by a long-standing interest in the history of the Hudson Valley.

Steamboat's Suit

Victoria Heckman

For Chic

Chicago, 1953

"I am a bagman for the mob," Penny said to herself as she wiped the counter at Pink's Candy and Soda Shoppe. She watched Steamboat as he moved from store to store across the street. The *real* bagman. She sighed. The closest she came to the mob was playing the numbers every Friday when she got her pay, in cash, in the little brown envelope labeled with her hours and wages, 35 cents an hour, from Edna, the accountant. Edna took the bets for the neighborhood. Because of that, Pink's didn't pay protection like the other businesses Steamboat was visiting today. The mob got a cut. They got a cut of everything that happened.

Penny knew a man who ran a furniture store who didn't pay protection. They slammed his leg in a door and broke his knee. She glanced at the clock and saw her day was over. She hung her apron up and got her purse from under the counter.

"Bye, Edna," she called. She heard an answering grunt from the back, and pushed out into the street. Although it was five o'clock, the day was still light. She walked along, paralleling Steamboat as he made his rounds.

He always looked so dapper. Dark suit and tie, the finest materials. She knew where he got his suits, Mr. Righetti's tailor shop. That's where her father occasionally had his suits made. They were expensive, but the best. Her father only got a new suit if something dire happened. A wedding. Or a funeral.

Steamboat didn't seem to notice her trailing along after

him. He just went into store after store, returning to the street almost immediately. The bag he carried didn't seem to get any bigger and Penny wondered about that. She also wondered why he didn't get mugged. I mean, week after week, he must carry around thousands of dollars. Steamboat was a big man, not really scary looking, but the temptation must be big to want to rob him. Crime was high here and although the mob ran a tight ship, someone always wanted to challenge the hierarchy.

Penny reached the corner where she turned toward her apartment house. She climbed the stairs to her family's walk up.

"Hi, Mom," she called as she hung her purse near her mother's in the entry hall. Her big brother Edward sat on the sofa reading the newspaper. Although he was only 17, two years older than Penny, he was huge. Bigger than their father who wasn't home from his own store, yet. The family owned a fruit and vegetable stand, that also specialized in Italian foods from Naples.

"How was work, dear?" Elena asked her daughter.

"Yeah, dear. How was work?" Edward echoed.

Penny threw a sofa pillow at him. "Fine. I'm hungry. When's dinner?"

"The same as always, Squirt," Edward said. "When Dad gets home."

Penny moved to the kitchen sink to wash her hands. "Not in the kitchen!" her mother exclaimed.

"Fine. I don't see why not."

"Penny, I tell you every day. You wash your hands at the other sink."

"Unless you're cooking," Penny finished.

"Unless you're cooking," Elena echoed. Penny washed her hands at the correct sink and began to set the table.

As she finished her father came home, slamming the door and whistling. A good day at the store.

"Hi, Papa!" Penny rushed to hug him. She was as tall as he was now. Antonio was a slim, dapper man who always wore a suit and tie to work. Once at the store, he carefully hung his jacket up, replaced it with his grocer's apron, then reversed the process at the end of the day.

Antonio hugged his daughter and kissed his wife. Edward was at that awkward stage, too old to hug, and too close to shake hands, so Antonio settled for a nod.

"Hi, Dad," Edward said without looking up from the paper.

"Wash up and come to the table," Elena said. Edward didn't move, but Antonio went to wash.

Penny finished serving at her mother's direction and by then Edward had wandered in from washing his hands and sat.

They said a blessing and Antonio began to serve and pass the dishes. "Thank you my dear," he said to his wife. "This looks delicious."

He always said the same thing. Penny smiled at her parents.

"I saw Steamboat today," she said.

"What was he doing?" Edward asked.

"Collecting!"

"It's best to mind your own business," Antonio said, "Things happen in this neighborhood." He exchanged a glance with his wife.

"What things?" Penny had heard the rumors of course, like everyone else. The shopkeepers who didn't pay, who bet numbers. Well, everyone bet numbers, even the kids. There were other rumors about what the mob did. Steamboat was the only real mobster she had ever seen and she kept a close eye on him when he came to the neighborhood. She had never spoken to him, she would be too nervous, but just working in a place where he came to get the money was so exciting!

"About Steamboat's bag," she began. She glanced up and all eyes were on her, even Edward's. "Um, it's so small. Why doesn't it get bigger if all he does is collect money all day?"

Her mother stood and began to clear the table. "Penny, that is dangerous talk."

Antonio wiped his mouth with a napkin. "We have to work and live in this neighborhood. My store is here because they *let* me be here. Do not stir things up. Do you still want to work at Pink's?"

"Yes." Penny wasn't sure why this had gotten so serious all of a sudden. It was just a question.

"Then you leave Steamboat and his business alone. I mean it. You go to work, you come home. That's it. Do you understand?" Antonio stood and went into her parents' bedroom.

Penny watched him go. "Yes," she whispered.

"You did it now, Squirt," Edward said. He also pushed away from the table and went back to reading the paper on the sofa.

Silently Penny and her mother cleaned up after the meal.

The next day was Friday and at the end of her shift, Penny received the brown envelope with her pay. She studied Edna. Teased dyed hair, cigarette dangling from her mouth, eyes squinting behind black framed glasses from the trail of smoke. Penny had never really looked at Edna before.

"What?" Edna did not like her staring.

"Oh, sorry, Edna. I was just thinking."

"Do it some where's else, I got things to do."

"Okay, bye Edna." Penny didn't move.

"What?" Edna said again, even more sharply.

"I just want to play my number."

"Fine. The usual?" She didn't wait for an answer. "Just leave it. I'll get to it."

Penny left the office. She walked toward the little lake front park nearby. The day was still warm and bright. What's going on with Steamboat? What's going on in the neighborhood? Her parents had seemed so tense last night when she asked about the bag. It was a reasonable question, wasn't it? Did he give money to someone on the way? That would make sense, so he wouldn't carry all that money around. Did people later on his rounds trade for larger denominations so he didn't have such a large volume to tote? That made sense, too. She was so curious, and now she wasn't even allowed to ask.

The park still had patrons in the nice weather and Penny sat and watched the lake and the kids playing while she thought about Steamboat. The sun dropped lower and she headed for home.

Saturdays Pink's stayed open late and she usually worked into the evening. She wasn't allowed to date, too young, but she worked and watched the young couples as they held hands and shared a soda with two straws. Someday, she would do that. When she was sixteen, she would be allowed to date. Edward was conscripted to walk her home after her late shifts on Saturdays. He complained endlessly about it, but truly didn't seem to mind unless he had a date of his own. That hadn't been often until about a month ago when he had begun seeing Dolores, a beautiful blonde who attended the Catholic high school. Now Edward sometimes met Dolores at Pink's so he could walk Penny home. Tonight, they came in near closing time and sat in a booth by the window. Penny was stationed at the soda fountain across from the window, the long counter that ran from the door to the back of the shop.

Edward approached the counter. "Two root beer floats."

"Okay." Penny made the floats and brought them to him where he waited at the counter.

"Hey, Squirt, I was wonderin'. Can you get home by yourself tonight?"

"You're supposed to walk me home."

"Yeah, I know, but it's only five blocks, and me and Dolores, we got plans."

"What kind of plans?" Penny knew what plans, since she had seen them kissing before.

Edward flushed. "Jeez, Squirt, just a little privacy. Please? And don't tell Mom or Dad."

Penny studied him as if thinking about it. She watched him squirm. "Okay, but you can't call me Squirt for a whole week."

Edward sighed in relief. "Thanks Squirt. I mean Penny. I'll see you later." He raced back to Dolores and hustled her out before Penny had time to put his money in the cash register. She finished her shift and closed up. Edna would do the register in the morning. She swept and cleared and then got her purse. She shut off the lights to the main store and locked the front door as she went out. It was late and all was quiet.

On the dark street she saw a familiar shadow. She thought it might be Edward, but he would be with Dolores. Unless something went wrong with his plans. She smirked a little at that thought as she watched the figure in a doorway across the way.It lurched out and she saw it was Steamboat, not Edward. Had he been drinking? He walked away, a little unsteady. Although it was in the opposite direction of home, she couldn't help herself. She followed. She stayed on her side of the street and next to the buildings. Steamboat made his way toward the park. He had just turned onto the sidewalk that ran along the park when two dark figures approached him and took an arm each, guiding him into the dark park.

Penny's breath caught. Her heart beat faster, but she couldn't stop herself from following. Steamboat was hers. Sort of. Her project, anyway. She wore a dark coat and her soft soled shoes and made almost no noise as she stayed well back. They were easy to see even though the park had no lights at night. It was narrow and long, following the lake front. The blob with Steamboat continued to the boat ramp. She could go no further because there was no place to hide between the edge of the park and the ramp itself. A small boat bobbed in the shallows.

The group approached the side of the boat and the figure of Steamboat suddenly sagged. The other two had to support him and he flopped into the boat. Penny gasped, not really knowing what she had seen, but understanding it all the same. The men were too far away to hear her. The sound of the engine starting masked the sound of her scurrying toward the park exit and the street.

The next few days passed and between church, work, and chores, Penny was busy, however she still could not get what she had seen out of her mind. Did she see what she thought she had? Her hobby of spying on Steamboat had been a game, but now. . .? She kept a watchful eye but by Wednesday she still had not seen Steamboat. Wednesday night her father asked if she wanted to pick up his new suit with him after he closed the shop the next day. She didn't work Thursday so she agreed.

"Good afternoon, Mr. Righetti," Antonio called to the elderly tailor when they entered his store.

"Good afternoon, Mr. Bennini. Young lady," he replied. "Yes, come right back and try this on. Young lady you wait here until we see how dashing your father look, okay?" Mr. Righetti's English was not quite as good as her parents'. She heard them discussing fitting and tailoring and other boring things. Her ears picked up when Mr. Righetti said, "Did you hear?"

In Penny's experience, that always meant something juicy would be said. Something she wasn't supposed to hear.

"What?" her father asked.

"They found Steamboat."

"Where?"

"In the lake. Cement shoes, you know."

"Oh, my,' her father mumbled.

Penny's heart sped up. She wiped her damp hands on her skirt.

Her father continued. "Do they know who?"

Mr. Righetti laughed. "Of course they know. Do they do anything about it? Of course not." He kept chuckling. "That's what happen when you dip into the bag that isn't yours. By the way, I got a new suit for Steamboat here. It too big for you, but it fit your Edward good. I make you a good deal. Steamboat sure not gonna need it now."

♦ ♦ ♦ ♦

Victoria Heckman's first *Hawai'i mystery series* features officer Katrina Ogden, K.O., of the Honolulu Police Department. Her second series, *Coconut Man mysteries of Ancient Hawai'i* begins with *Kapu-Sacred*. Her newest work, *Burn Out,* is a stand alone mystery starring animal communicator Elizabeth Murphy. She is president of the Central Coast Chapter of Sisters in Crime. Visit her website http://www.victoriaheckman.com or email her at vheckman@charter.net

A Sojourn At The Coast

D.K. Farris

My Dearest Sister:

I write to inform you that my domestic arrangements have again changed, albeit temporarily. When last I wrote to you, I had recently departed my room over a saloon on Pacific Street for the more cultivated atmosphere of a suite in the Palace Hotel. (A four-day poker game with several young men of rich parentage and poor judgment can do wonders for one's worldly circumstances.) The differences between Franklin's Saloon and the Palace Hotel are thus: the liquor is finer, the harlots are called "debutantes" and the thieves are better dressed.

A shortness of breath and recurring dyspepsia proved a great enough annoyance that I actually took counsel other than my own. It was the opinion of a physician from Boston and an arborist from Venezuela (to whom I paid less money and more heed) that my health would improve with a restful retreat in the sea air. I pointed out to them that San Francisco has sea air in plenitude, since the city is on a peninsula and is ably supplied with said sea air from both the Pacific Ocean and the San Francisco Bay. They, in turn, pointed out to me, that the sea air in another locale may have a lower concentration of whiskey fumes, tobacco smoke and the various scented "Eau"s that both sexes in the City habitually apply. So I have repaired to a place with plentiful sea air, which I must leaven with my own whiskey fumes and tobacco smoke. The "Eau"s I have left behind, and gladly. Indeed, I find few things more off-putting than a Titan of Finance who smells like a hogshead of magnolias.

Determined to restore myself to the peak of health, I packed a satchel with clean socks and fresh shirt collars, and a steamer trunk with brandy, whiskey, cigars, playing cards and other essentials, and struck out southward in search of more salubrious climes. After a journey of a few days, utilizing every conveyance known to man other than, perhaps, the Finnish Dog-Cart, I arrived here. "Here" is the town of San Luis Obispo where I have rented a small cottage. This place shares a history with a number of other towns in California. Some hundred-odd years ago a plucky band of Spanish explorers came up from what was then New Spain to settle in the untenanted wilderness. The fact that the place had been peaceably inhabited for hundreds of years by a tribe of Red Indians called the Choo-mash was of no moment, for the Choo-mash were Savage Heathens. Their Savagery was evidenced by the fact that they did not wear trousers or live in houses with brass door-knockers. Their Heathen status was confirmed in that they did not perform their religious observances in a building with a bell on the roof. That the Choo-mash dressed sensibly and modestly by their own lights, that their homes were constructed to their needs and that their Devotions were agreeable to their own Manifestation of Divinity notwithstanding, the Spaniard undertook to Civilize them.

Perhaps the greatest Sin of all is that of Minding One's Own Business, for when Civilized folk come upon a band of people Minding Their Own Business, their first order of business is to fall upon those people and Mend Their Ways. Perhaps I imbue the Red Indians with virtues they do not possess. Perhaps, had the Indians discovered powder, shot and the sailing ship first, the great cities of Europe would now be awash with Choo-mash missionaries exhorting the populace to abandon their foolish Christian superstitions and embrace the True Faith of the Bear God or the Sky Spirit.

In any event, the Choo-mash became Mission Indians, speaking the Spanish tongue, tilling Spanish crops, wearing Spanish clothes and praying to the Spanish God. They also adopted

Spanish vices and caught Spanish diseases, their numbers dwindling with every generation as Civilization took its toll. The Choo-mash remained Mission Indians after Mexico broke away from Spain and the Missions were largely cast adrift. Secularly, the result of the War of Independence caused little more than a change in the bunting adorning the top of the town flagpole. The Great Excitement of '48 and the subsequent admission of California as a state of the Union had similar effects on the town, the Mission, the Mission Indians and the bunting atop the flagpole.

I mention all this because upon arrival here I became acquainted with one of the Mission Indians. He was recommended to me as a sober, industrious and trustworthy fellow who did odd jobs about town and would "look after" me for a small retainer. Thus, I engaged him to keep the larder stocked with coffee, bacon, butter, fresh eggs and suchlike. Most important of his duties was to bring me the day's newspaper as it left the press. Even after all these years, I love the scent of fresh ink.

Most often, when a fellow is recommended to a newcomer as being "sober, industrious and trustworthy," he is none of the aforementioned, but rather possesses the solitary virtue of being a relative of the speaker. Not so the case with Tomas (pronounced in the Spanish fashion as "toe-MOSS" rather than the Yankee-style "tommus." I include this information, since I believe you have little acquaintance with Mission Indians in Connecticut, but perhaps I am wrong.) Tomas is, indeed, possessed of the advertised virtues and I feel confident in leaving mundane affairs in his hands as I engage in the more rarefied of the local pursuits such as arguing politics with the cracker barrel philosophers, shying walnuts at crows, and attempting to find a locally produced wine that won't kill an Army mule at twenty paces.

I hold little hope for the latter, for although the Spaniards brought the grape with them, this region is utterly unsuitable for winemaking. This does not, however, dissuade the locals from making what they refer to as wine, a grape-based intoxicant approximating boot polish thinned with turpentine. The one virtue the stuff possesses is that a few pennies will purchase a gallon of the stuff, allowing the impecunious to join the inebriated.

One of those most reliant on this vile potion is a local fellow named Steve Hardiker. He is Tomas' mirror-twin, for every one of Tomas' virtues, Hardiker has cultivated a sympathetic vice. Where Tomas is abstemious of drink, Hardiker is infrequently seen without a skinful. Where Tomas is diligent and industrious, Hardiker is the second-best harness mender in town, and in a town this small, second-best is synonymous with worthless. Whereas Tomas is trustworthy, upon shaking hands with Hardiker, one would be well served to count one's fingers. Nonetheless, as a white man, Hardiker counts himself superior to Tomas in every way by virtue of accident of birth. When well in his cups, Hardiker will wave about a large clasp-knife and announce himself ready and willing to carve up any Indian, Chinaman, Mexican or Negro who "dast cross him or speak agin him." He seems to have cultivated an especially deep hatred of Tomas, asserting that "that filthy Injun" will revert to savagery and scalp us all in our beds. I cannot say that Steve Hardiker is the most loathsome man on Earth, but that is merely because I haven't yet met every other man on Earth.

Ah well. Enough of this. Evening is drawing nigh, so I shall walk down to Palm Street, where the Chinese congregate, to take my supper. Living in San Francisco I developed an appreciation of their victuals, finding them to be nourishing, plentiful and cheap. However, their spicing and preparation are quite different from ours, so I don't believe that Chinese cuisine will ever catch on.

And so, I remain,

Your Loving Brother

My Dearest Sister:

Today I undertook an expedition to seek out the much-touted sea air and test its ameliorative effects. San Luis Obispo is not, in fact, on the seacoast at all but some ten miles inland. The sea itself meets the great State of California at a tiny harbor known as Morro Bay. The bay is named for its most prominent feature, Morro Rock. This prominence is an enormous domed excrescence of some hard black stone that rises from the sea just offshore. Some Spanish punster named it El Moro for it bears a passing resemblance to a Moor's turbaned head, and "moro" is also the Spanish word for "pebble." I suppose if I were trapped aboard a creaking, leaking galleon for months on end, I, too, would seize any opportunity for amusement.

Morro Bay has little to recommend it, other than the aforementioned sea air and the opportunity to observe a large stone. It isn't really a bay at all, but a small lagoon, with nothing separating it from the open ocean except for what the locals are pleased to call The Spit, nothing more than a sand dune with delusions of grandeur. Legend has it that the Spaniards used this place as a freight harbor in its unimproved state for centuries, but it wasn't until some few years ago that a fellow named Riley built a great wooden longshore to facilitate lading. Indeed, this part of California, for all its barren appearance, produces a variety of goods in quantities to make a modern facility a paying concern.

At first I contemplated hiring a trap and driving myself to the shore, but that seemed an affront to my generally slothful nature, so I purchased a bucket of beer and sought out a drayer bound for the seaport. The result was a pleasant journey, for he proved an affable man, and the sharing of beer again proved its time-honored reputation for building good fellowship. A couple of hours watching fishing boats go about their business and wharfies wrestle with bales, bundles and barrels of diverse sorts provided me with all the entertainment and sea air I could stand, so I found another thirsty drayer and jolted my way home again. I don't know whether it was the sea air or the beer but I do feel recovered.

As I was writing to you earlier tonight, there arose a great clamor and I went outside to see the cause. The cause was apparent, for a building was well afire a few blocks away. By the time I got there, the Fire Brigade was at work. There was little to do for the building itself, for every stick of it was ablaze, so the Brigade's duties were to keep the fire from spreading and reducing the whole town to ashes as happened in Chicago not all that long ago.

From people in the crowd I learned that the building was Steve Hardiker's place where he lived and worked, and I must admit I got a certain sense of satisfaction at watching that wretched man's business, home and worldly goods spiral away in a great plume of smoke. When the fire died down and the Brigade was wetting the embers, I returned home to this letter and to bed.

More events of great moment. Fortified with coffee and ajitter with curiosity, I made my way downtown this morning to acquaint myself with developments. First came the news that in the ruins of his workshop, Hardiker's badly charred remains had been discovered, with one of his own leather knives buried to the hilt in his chest. Apparently he was slain, and the fire set in an attempt to cover the murder. As for who would want Steve Hardiker dead, we must consult the Census Office for a full list.

The second newsworthy event was the report that the church at the Mission had been entered and ransacked during the night, perhaps while the entire populace was preoccupied with the fire. A small amount of cash money from offerings and the Poor Box was missing, and the cabinet containing all the silver vessels and implements necessary for services had been forced open and emptied.

As this news was yet circulating there came word of a most gruesome nature from the doctor who examined Hardiker's remains. Although Hardiker's flesh was badly charred and in places consumed by the fire, the doctor determined that the man had been scalped and the last finger of his left hand had been severed as some sort of grisly trophy before the corpse was set alight. San Luis Obispo, like any other town, including your own Hartford, is hardly innocent of crime, even murder. In this instance, however, the horror of the murder and mutilation of Hardiker and the subsequent arson which endangered the entire town whipped the populace to a frenzy bordering on madness.

It was not until early evening that I heard the final piece of news, to me, the most shocking of all. It seems that shortly after daybreak, a farmer found my own Tomas in one of his outbuildings. Discarding the wildest of rumors and more extravagant of claims, it seems that Tomas was found in a drunken stupor, and his shirt was spattered with blood and streaked with wine. He reportedly smelled quite strongly of kerosene as well as spirits. Finally, in his pockets were found a quantity of Chinese coins and even more damning, some small scraps of ornately worked silver which had obviously been wrenched from larger objects.

The farmer, knowing nothing of the night's events, simply rode into town and informed the town marshal that he had found a drunkard of suspicious appearance on his property. The town marshal, demonstrating far more sense than I ever credited him with, smuggled the still-groggy Tomas into town and had him safely in the jail before anyone knew he had been found. The townsfolk, more than a few of whom I knew, coalesced into a mob. This mob, hearing of the Chinese coins, and frustrated by the inaccessibility of Tomas himself, went through Chinatown in a barbarous fashion attempting to discover if any of the merchants had purchased the altar silver. They destroyed property and visited violence upon Chinese shopkeepers, finding no trace of the missing silver. The rampage took the keenest edge from their bloodlust, and they were further mollified, at least temporarily, with the promise of a speedy trial, which is set to begin Monday after next, less than ten days away.

I fear that Tomas is done for. For all that I liked Tomas and detested Hardiker, the evidence is overwhelming. Tomas himself can offer no explanation for the facts, claiming that he has no knowledge of any of the events of Friday night, or of how he came to be found in such compromising circumstances. Even were the circumstances totally different, perhaps a witnessed, clear-cut case of self-defense, I fear the trial of an Indian killing a white man could only end one way. I fear that his legal representation will be halfhearted at best, since his lawyer will be forcibly dragged into the traces by judicial order, and will be as anxious to see Tomas swing as any other townsman.

So, my dear sister, I conclude with heavy heart. A good man shall hang for ridding the world of a vile man.

Your Loving Brother

My Dearest Sister:

I received your letter this afternoon, and I must say the fact you sent it via Express stirred in me a pang of fear, for my first thought was that you had resorted to such means to inform me of a calamity in the family. I was quite surprised, at first, that you had gone to such measures over the case of Tomas, the Mission Indian. Then I recalled that in matters of Justice you are more fierce than Pallas Athena, armed, armored, and presented on the half-skull. To my credit, I had not forgotten this, I had merely poorly-remembered.

I read your letter carefully and several times over before I fully comprehended your purpose. I finally perceived that you had formulated each question most carefully, and then ordered those questions with a precision which would make a Logician from the Golden Age of Greece gasp with admiration. Once I apprehended your purpose, I set about finding the answers to those questions in the order you presented them.

To the first. The body was very badly burned and was identified as Steve Hardiker by virtue of it being a man's body of the proper height and build, discovered in Hardiker's place in the late hours of the night, and by the presence upon the body of certain imperishable objects of Hardiker's. Chief among these were a large, ornate nickel harness buckle which Hardiker used on his trouser belt and a small Turkish coin many recognized as an object habitually carried as his Lucky Piece. The second question, corollary to the first, had me puzzled at first sight, but its purpose soon became clear. The most significant of Hardiker's personal possessions which was NOT found upon the body was his infamous clasp-knife, from which he seemed inseparable.

To answer your next question, I walked down to the site of Hardiker's demise to see for myself what remains of the building. As you speculated in your query, the wood in the immediate vicinity of where the body lay was the most severely burned, some of it reduced completely to a fine white ash. The farther away from the body's location, the less fully was the wood burned. This caused me to deduce, as I am sure you had intended, that the arsonist's intent was to visit the full fury of the fire's destruction upon the corpse itself.

Following your list, I then proceeded to make inquiries about town. I jotted figures down on a scrap of foolscap as I went, then totted them up as I took my luncheon. As I am sure you suspected, between cash loans of varying amounts from individual persons and unpaid accounts to businesses, Hardiker's debts far exceeded his means. I was by no means thorough in my canvass, but the figure I arrived at indicated he owed at least five times the most generous estimation of his total worth, lock, stock and barrel.

Simultaneously with my inquiries about Hardiker's finances, I asked, as you directed, about the sudden absence of people of little note. I heard nothing which piqued my interest in my perambulations, so I resolved to quest further afield. To this end I hired a fast gig with a smart horse and hastened to the harbor at Morro Bay. There, among the fishing boats, I heard of two men who had been paid in the early afternoon of that fateful Friday and had not been seen since. This aroused no notice, for on payday sailors and fishermen are like thistledown on the wind. One of the absent was described as a small, wiry Portuguese, but the other was a Swede of the same frame as Hardiker. The captain said his name was Jensen or Jansen, but he was nicknamed 'Ninepins' for he was missing the last finger on his left hand.

Like the Pharos at Alexandria, your intellect has sundered the darkness from afar. I finally apprehended the truth of the matter. I drove back into town, surrendered the gig and immediately dispatched a series of letters to certain acquaintances of mine in San Francisco who are of an entrepreneurial inclination. One question as yet unanswered in my mind, was how could a lifelong abstainer such as Tomas be found in such an obvious state of inebriation? I had an inspiration and stopped by the Chinese mercantile owned by Ah Louis, a local bigwig, to ask a couple of questions. He confirmed my suspicions by telling me that despite Hardiker's oft-voiced opinion that the Chinese are naught but "yellow monkeys," Hardiker entered Ah Louis' shop and purchased a small number of opium balls that Friday afternoon. Ah Louis told me that an opium ball crushed into highly spiced food, such as is favored by Mexicans and Mission Indians, would be undetectable and in sufficient quantity would render a grown man insensible for many hours. As an afterthought, he mentioned that the town marshal had asked him to examine the coins found in Tomas' possession. It seems these coins, though numerous, had a total value of less than three American dollars, hardly the value of even one piece of worked silver.

Some days later two of my correspondents replied to my inquiries with the information that certain others in the same line of work had been approached by a travel-stained and singularly unpleasant white man attempting to sell some silver liturgical goods. Neither of these purveyors of undocumented valuables knew whether this "Mr. Lee," as he styled himself, had found a purchaser for his silver, or, indeed, whether this "Mr. Lee" was still in San Francisco.

As you have doubtless concluded, your illuminating letter, with its intriguing sequence of questions, arrived well after Tomas' intemperately early trial date, inevitable conviction, and hastily-scheduled execution. Allow me to ease your anguish, gentle sister, by relating to you a series of peculiar events which occurred a few days after my last letter. I shall relate these events in, more or less, chronological order and shall never comment upon them beyond what is set out below.

The first peculiar event took place in the afternoon of the Thursday before Tomas' trial. The night jailor, a fellow of reduced means, and noted for his poor luck, had a sudden reversal of fortune. He chanced to stop in a saloon bar for refreshment, and happened to enter a friendly game of Texas Poker with a visitor from San Francisco. Demonstrating a heretofore unnoticed skill for the game, and a dazzling run of luck, he, in full view of the public, managed, in just under three hours, to win precisely one thousand dollars.

The second peculiar event was that on that very night, the same night jailor was attending his duties when he was attacked. Apparently, a gang of desperadoes crept up behind him, struck him insensible, and locked him, trussed like a roasting fowl, into a cell, and spirited Tomas away. Rumors flying about town assign responsibility for this act to Mexican Banditos, Renegade Indians, China Sea Pirates, the Freemasons, the Rosicrucians, Gypsies and an itinerant band of Whirling Dervishes.

Sturdy man that he is, the night jailor recovered from the injuries to his dignity and to his skull with an admirable celerity. So swift and complete was his recovery, that, on that afternoon, he felt himself constitutionally revived enough to venture to a well-frequented saloon bar for some refreshment. After repeating his tale of peril several times to the spellbound habitués, he chanced to meet the visitor from San Francisco. On the offer of a rematch by the visitor, the night jailor demonstrated the completeness of his recovery by winning, in full public view, another one thousand dollars.

At about the same time a freshening wind bore a schooner laden with barrels of salted beef and corrosive wine, destined for Ecuador and points further south, out of the harbor at Morro Bay. This vessel left port with one more deckhand than with which it had arrived. This new fellow, whose name was quite illegible on the ship's papers, was ignorant of all things nautical. As such, he was accounted an Apprentice Seaman. The costs of his Apprenticeship were defrayed by some sixty freshly minted gold double-eagles, conveyed to the ship's Captain in a plain brown leather poke by a person of so little distinction that I am sure said Captain will find himself utterly unable to recall anything at all of the man, were he ever to be asked.

On to other things. I shall leave this place and go back to San Francisco, hopefully to find an unengaged room over the saloon of the ever-hospitable Mr. Franklin. One of the reasons for my departure is the revulsion I feel seeing bland, friendly expressions on faces that I had seen contorted in mindless rage so little time ago. The other reason is that I seem to find myself short of funds. My winnings of earlier this year are greatly diminished, and of the money remaining, some eight hundred dollars and three cents must be held for necessary expenditures. Five hundred of those dollars must be ready to instantly place in the hand of the person who informs me of the current whereabouts of Steve Hardiker. Another three hundred is earmarked for the expenses attendant upon securing the fastest possible means of conveyance there. The three cents is the cost of a pistol cartridge.

I remain,

Your Loving Brother

D. K. Farris is a native Californian, born in San Diego and now residing in the Mother Lode area of the Sierras. As a historical reenactor of both the Elizabethan Era and the California Gold Rush period, he is more comfortable in times other than his own. He began writing after being driven beyond the brink of madness by the success of his sister, crime fiction author Victoria Heckman.

www.ingramcontent.com/pod-product-compliance
Lightning Source LLC
Chambersburg PA
CBHW020803250626
47155CB00003B/1181